Praise for *Cousins*

"A novel of depraved genius."　　—ENRIQUE VILA-MATAS

"*Cousins* is a novel that makes you laugh out loud with its provocations and unexpected choices. Bodies are pushed to the limit in writing that gushes forth like blood. With *Cousins*, Aurora Venturini achieved the acclaim she'd been seeking all her life and enjoyed it in characteristic fashion: baring the scars of the monstrous persona she cultivated with ironic lucidity."
—MARIANA ENRIQUEZ, author of *Things We Lost in the Fire*

"Brimming with life, humor, and a vital twist of darkness, Venturini's English-language debut marks the arrival of a singular voice with a sharp, visceral approach to story. Reading *Cousins* is like being inside the belly of a wild, rambunctious beast, going where it goes, exhilarated no matter how perilous the journey."　　—ALEXANDRA KLEEMAN, author of *Something New Under the Sun*

"Cruel and strange and colorful—*Cousins* will be an immediate favorite for fans of Fleur Jaeggy and Leonora Carrington."
—CATHERINE LACEY, author of *Biography of X* and *Pew*

Cousins

Cousins

A Novel

Aurora Venturini

TRANSLATED FROM THE SPANISH BY KIT MAUDE

WITH AN INTRODUCTION BY MARIANA ENRIQUEZ

Soft Skull
New York

First Soft Skull Press edition: 2023

Library of Congress Cataloging-in-Publication Data
Names: Venturini, Aurora, author. | Maude, Kit, translator. |
Enriquez, Mariana, writer of introduction.
Title: Cousins : a novel / Aurora Venturini ; translated from the Spanish by Kit Maude ; with an introduction by Mariana Enriquez. Other titles: Primas. English
Description: First Soft Skull Press edition. | New York : Soft Skull, 2023.
Identifiers: LCCN 2022047292 | ISBN 9781593767297 (trade paperback) | ISBN 9781593767303 (ebook)
Subjects: LCGFT: Novels.
Classification: LCC PQ7797.V4214 P7513 2023 |
DDC 863/.64—dc23/eng/20221208
LC record available at https://lccn.loc.gov/2022047292

Cover design by Nicole Caputo
Book design by Wah-Ming Chang

Published by Soft Skull Press
New York, NY
www.softskull.com

Printed in the United States of America

1 3 5 7 9 10 8 6 4 2

Introduction

It was cold, or so my unreliable memory tells me. I was reading in bed with a mug of coffee on the nightstand. The floor was covered with ring-bound entries to the *Página/12* newspaper's New Novel competition for which I was working as a preliminary juror, narrowing down the selection for consideration by the jury proper. The manuscript for *Las primas* was very different from the others. For a start, it was typewritten—unusual enough by 2007—and to correct her mistakes the author had used liquid paper that in places had spread over neighboring words as well, but it was still legible. My first encounter with the narrator of *Las primas* came as a shock. Her radical syntax, which abhorred punctuation because it "exhausted" her, her brutal descriptions of the characters' miseries, her breathtaking mercilessness toward her family. "We were unusual which is to say we weren't normal," says Yuna, the narrator, a young woman with cognitive difficulties (Aurora would never say something so politically correct; she'd say Yuna was a half-wit), whose sister Betina is bound to a wheelchair by severe physical and mental disabilities and sometimes needs to be cared for at a specialized institution. Yuna calls it a Cottolengo, which is where difficult cases such as her sister were generally sent. It was when I got to one of the scenes set there that I was first moved to ask myself, almost out loud: "What on earth is this? Who wrote this book? What's it about?" The scene goes like this:

> As I waited for Betina's class to finish, I walked around the corridors of the coven. I saw a priest come in accompanied by an altar boy. Someone had given him a sheet, a soul. The priest sprinkled holy water and said that if you have a soul God welcomes you to his bosom.
>
> To what or whom was he talking?
>
> I went closer and saw a prominent family from Adrogué. On the table I saw a cannelloni sitting on top of a silk cushion. It wasn't a cannelloni but something that had come out of a human womb, otherwise the priest wouldn't have baptized it.

I made inquiries and a nurse told me that every year the distinguished couple brought a cannelloni to be baptized. The doctor had advised the mother not to give birth anymore because there was nothing to be done. But they said that as good Catholics they had to procreate. In spite of my handicap I knew that this was disgusting but I couldn't say so. That night I felt so sick I couldn't eat.

I finished the novel and I think the very next day I called Liliana Viola, another of the pre-jurors, to discuss my surprise, my confusion, my admiration. Was this a brilliant novel? What was so brilliant about it? The risks it takes? The eccentricity? The fact that I'd never seen anything like it? The voice from out of nowhere? Who might the author be? Liliana had read *Las primas* too and was in a similar state, torn between fascination and bewilderment. I think we both knew that if the jury recognized how radical the text and story were, it would have a good chance of winning. And so it did.

Aurora Venturini was eighty-five years old when she won *Página/12*'s New Novel Award. She turned up to the award ceremony with a punk attitude; she had a skinny frame with unusual features arranged into an expression set somewhere between amusement and candor—her dark, peering eyes, meanwhile, were more like malevolent slits—declaring: "Finally, an honest jury." She had published dozens of books, was a supporter of the Peronist movement, friend of Evita, and went into exile in Paris following the coup of 1955. In France she became friends with Violette Leduc and socialized with existentialists. Myths gathered around her and she actively encouraged them during her lifetime: Aurora saw ghosts from a young age, she was friendly with Victoria Ocampo and Borges when she lived in Buenos Aires (when not in exile she spent seventeen years there and the rest of her life in La Plata); she was an obsessive writer and kept spiders as pets. When she fell out of bed and was taken to the hospital with broken bones she visited hell and after that made friends with an exorcist priest. How much of this was true wasn't remotely important, among other things because her books are so authentic. Most of them were published by independent presses or as winners of municipal prizes and all of them are odd and obsessed with one subject in particular: family.

Las primas is a story about family, and about women. It is, Aurora said, an autobiographical novel. "I'm not very family-oriented, I never was, but I always end up writing about my family, or families. My creations are all freaks. My family was very freakish. It's what I know. I'm not very ordinary. I'm a strange creature who only wants to write. I'm not very sociable. I only ever see people on December 24." *Las primas* is the monologue of a half-wit but it's not full of rage, but rather bewilderment and, above all, disgust. The men of the family are absent: the male characters who do appear are abusive and ravage the bodies of vulnerable women with the indifference of petty scoundrels. The story is set in the forties: the mother is a high-ranking primary school teacher, a prestigious role for a woman but also one of the few available. Yuna manages to escape the house, in her mind at least, because she is a painter. She has talent and is helped by a professor who convinces her to study at art school and exhibit her work. And yet she is forever bound to the suffering bodies of the women of the family, her aunt Nené, her cousins Carina and Petra, and the mild-mannered Rufina in the darkness of a gloomy suburban house where Betina wheels around harumming and drooling. "I painted shadows which I couldn't help because I have so many shadows inside me that when I get overwrought (idem) I drive them out onto my paintings." That "idem" refers to the use of a word (*overwrought*) that Yuna has looked up in the dictionary because she has a meager vocabulary. She writes against language, against writing conventions, getting the best she can out of her precarious oral skills. In this struggling voice Yuna describes not just her own coming of age but also those of the other girls, all of whom are used and neglected. The first to suffer abuse is Carina, one of the cousins: she is impregnated by a neighbor (a "potato man," or greengrocer) and Aunt Nené decides that she has to get an abortion. There aren't many abortions in Argentine literature and here we're given a vivid account of the shoddiness that comes with illegality:

> The doctor came but she didn't look like one she looked common. She asked which the patient was and how many months and Aunt Nené answered three-and-change and I understood why people say that children bring good luck but Aunt Nené who didn't eat every day for lack of money wouldn't pardon the baby even with the change it brought. Come in said the doctor and Carina went inside trembling, she asked if her aunt could come too and the doctor said no and closed the door to the other room. The metallic screech of the equipment grew more shrill.

Carina's abortion doesn't end well, but we won't reveal any more here other than that Petra, Carina's sister, a Lilliputian young woman who starts to work as a prostitute as a teenager, will get her revenge. The cousins Yuna and Petra band together to try to put an end to the chain of abuse from which they, too, have suffered but nothing is ever enough in this pessimistic, brutal novel with no out-and-out heroines, a novel of extreme, sickly, obsessive, mistreated women. Aurora Venturini loved black humor, cruelty, and monstrosity: she considered herself to be an anomaly and believed in a twisted but playful approach to literature. *Las primas* is a novel that makes you laugh out loud with its provocations and unexpected choices. Bodies are pushed to the limit in writing that gushes forth like blood. With *Las primas* Aurora Venturini achieved the acclaim she'd been seeking all her life and enjoyed it in characteristic fashion: baring the scars of the monstrous persona she cultivated with ironic lucidity.

—MARIANA ENRIQUEZ

Cousins

Part One

A Handicapped Childhood

My mother was a teacher with a white uniform and pointer, she was very strict but taught well at a school in the suburbs for not very bright children from the middle classes and below. The smartest was Rubén Fiorlandi, the grocer's son. My mother smacked naughty children over the head with her pointer and sent them to sit in the corner wearing donkey's ears she'd made out of colored cardboard. They rarely acted up twice. My mother believed that one learned nothing if the rod was spared. The children in the third grade called her the Third Grade Miss even though she was married to my father who left her and never came back to perform his duties as paterfamilias. She did her teaching work in the morning and returned home at two in the afternoon. Lunch had already been prepared by Rufina, the northern girl who was our very diligent housekeeper and knew how to cook. I was sick of stew every day. Out back clucked a henhouse that laid for us and in the garden miraculously golden squashes sprouted suns dislodged from their celestial home and fallen to earth, growing next to violets and scrawny rosebushes nobody bothered to take care of but that insisted on adding their perfume to our dingy hovel anyway.

I've never told anyone but I only learned to tell the time from clock faces at the age of twenty. I'm surprised and embarrassed to confess it now. Surprised and embarrassed because of what it will tell you about me and I start to remember all kinds of questions. The question I remember most particularly is: What time is it? The truth was that I didn't know the time and I was as horrified by clocks as I was by my sister's orthopedic wheelchair.

She was stupider than me but she knew how to read clock faces. Not books though. We were unusual which is to say we weren't normal.

Harummm . . . harummm . . . harummm . . . babbled Betina, my sister, as she wheeled her bad luck around the little garden and flagstones of the patio. Her harums were choked with drool, the dodo drooled. Poor Betina. She was a mistake of nature. Poor me, another mistake, and poor mother who was burdened with both abandonment and freaks.

But anything goes in this filthy world of ours. So there's no use feeling too sorry for anyone or anything.

Sometimes I think that we're a dream or a nightmare that plays out day after day but at any given moment will cease to be, vanish from the sheet of our souls and torture us no longer.

Betina Has an Emotional Disorder

That was the psychologist's diagnosis. I don't know if I've written it right. My sister suffered from a curved spine, from behind sitting down she looked like a hunchback with stubby legs and extraordinary arms. The old woman who came to darn socks said that mother must have had some harm done to her during pregnancy, worse with Betina.

I asked the psychologist, a woman with hair on her lip and a monobrow, what *emotional* meant.

She answered that it had to do with your soul, but I was too young to understand. Still I guessed that a soul was like a white sheet inside our bodies and when it got stained it made people stupid, like Betina and a little like me.

As Betina circled the table harummming away, I noticed a

little tail poking out through the gap between the back and seat of the orthopedic chair and said to myself that it must be her soul slipping out.

I asked the psychologist another question this time whether the soul had to do with life and she said that it did, and then added that when it went away people died and the soul went to heaven if they'd been good or hell if they'd been bad.

Harummm . . . harummm . . . harummm . . . she continued to drag her soul behind her and I saw it growing longer every day encrusted with gray lumps and so assumed that it would be falling off soon and Betina would die. But I didn't care because she disgusted me.

At mealtimes I had to feed my sister and missed her mouth on purpose and shoved the spoon in her eye, her ear, up her nose before it got to her gaping maw. Ah . . . ah . . . ah . . . sniveled the dirty creature.

I grabbed her by the hair and shoved her face into her food and that would shut her up. I wasn't to blame for my parents' mistakes. I considered stamping on her soul tail. But the story about hell stopped me.

I had read the catechism at mass and "thou shalt not kill" had been seared into me. But a little tap here and a little tap there and the tail no one else could see grew and grew. Only I could see it and I was thrilled.

Schools of Alternative Education

I wheeled Betina to her school. Then I walked to mine. Betina's school dealt with serious cases. Like Pig Boy with his piggy snout, jowls, and ears who ate from a gold plate and drank broth from a gold cup. He grabbed the cup with his chubby, cloven trotters and slurped like water splashing into a pit and when he ate solid food he waggled his jaws and ears but his teeth were useless, they stuck out like a wild boar's. He looked at me once. Beady eyes, a pair of inexpressive balls buried in fat, but they kept looking at me and I stuck out my tongue so he grunted and threw down his tray. The carers came and had to calm him down, trussing him up like an animal, which is what he was.

As I waited for Betina's class to finish, I walked around the corridors of the coven. I saw a priest come in accompanied by an altar boy. Someone had given him a sheet, a soul. The priest sprinkled holy water and said that if you have a soul God welcomes you to his bosom.

To what or whom was he talking?

I went closer and saw a prominent family from Adrogué. On the table I saw a cannelloni sitting on top of a silk cushion. It wasn't a cannelloni but something that had come out of a human womb, otherwise the priest wouldn't have baptized it.

I made inquiries and a nurse told me that every year the distinguished couple brought a cannelloni to be baptized. The doctor had advised the mother not to give birth anymore because there was nothing to be done. But they said that as good Catholics they had to procreate. In spite of my handicap I knew that this was disgusting but I couldn't say so. That night I felt so sick I couldn't eat.

My sister's soul kept on growing. I was glad that my father had left.

Development

Betina was eleven and I was twelve. Rufina declared, They're at the age of development, and I imagined something coming out of me and prayed to Saint Teresita for it not to be a cannelloni. I asked the psychologist what *development* meant and she went red in the face and told me to ask my mother.

My mother went red in the face too and said that at a certain age girls stopped being girls and became young ladies. Then she stopped talking and I was left wondering.

I've already said that I went to a school for the handicapped, but not as handicapped as Betina's. A girl said that she was developed. I didn't see anything different about her. She told me that what happens is you bleed from between your legs for a few days and you have to use a pad to stop your clothes getting stained and be careful with boys because you can get pregnant.

That night I couldn't get to sleep. I felt around the area in question, but it wasn't damp so I could still talk to boys. When I did develop I would never go near a boy I didn't want to get pregnant and have a cannelloni or anything like it.

Betina talked a lot, or rather she mumbled and made herself understood. One evening during a family gathering that we weren't allowed to attend because we didn't have good enough manners, especially at mealtimes, my sister cried in her booming voice: Mommy, I'm bleeding from my privates. We were in the room next door to the one where the festivities were being held. A grandma and two cousins came.

I told the cousins not to get too close to the bleeder because they might make her pregnant.

They all left offended and Mother hit us both with her pointer.

I went to school and told them that Betina was developed even though she was younger than me. The teacher told me off. We weren't to discuss immoral things in the classroom and she failed me in Morals and Citizenship. The class became a bunch of worriers, especially the girls who occasionally touched themselves feeling for potential dampness.

I stopped associating with boys just in case.

One afternoon Margarita came in grinning and said it came and we all knew what she meant.

My sister abandoned her schooling in the third grade. It was no use. Really it wasn't any use for either of us and I left in the sixth grade. Yes, I learned to read and write, but the latter with spelling errors and I never write the silent letters because what's the point in them?

The psychologist said that I read with a lisp. But she thought that if I practiced I would get better and forced me to say tongue twisters like Peter Piper pecked a pick of pickled peppers if Peter Piper pecked a pick of pickled peppers how many pickled peppers did Peter Piper pick?

Mother watched and when I couldn't overcome my lisp she hit me on the head with her pointer. The psychologist forbade Mother from being there during the Peter Piper and I got better because when Mother was there I rushed the Peter Piper out of fear of the pointer.

Betina harummed around, opening her mouth and pointing to it because she was hungry.

I didn't like to eat at the same table as Betina. It was disgusting. She drank her soup straight from the bowl without a spoon and ate solids with her hands. She cried when I insisted on feeding her because of how I wasn't particular about which orifice the spoon was shoved into.

They bought Betina a high chair with an enamel tray and

a hole in the seat for defecation and pee. She'd go during meal-times. The smell made me sick. Mother warned me not to be prissy or she'd send me to the Cottolengo. I knew that the Cot-tolengo was a home for the handicapped and so my meals were, you might say, accompanied by the perfume of my sister's poo and showers of piss. I pinched her when she farted.

After meals I went out to the garden.

Rufina cleaned Betina and put her in her orthopedic chair. The dumbo napped with her chin on her chest, or rather her breasts because two fairly round lumps already poked out from beneath her clothes taunting me because she had developed before me and disgusting as she was a young lady before me which meant that Rufina had to change her pads every month and wash between her legs.

I could take care of myself and noticed that my breasts didn't grow because I was skinny as a beanpole or Mother's pointer. And so birthdays came and went but I started taking a drawing and painting class and the professor at the School of Fine Art said that I would be a major artist because I was half-crazy and drew and painted like the flamboyant artists of recent times.

The Exhibition at

the School of Fine Art

The professor said: "Yuna," which is my name, "your paintings are worthy of an exhibition. Someone might even want to buy them."

I was so happy that I jumped on top of the professor with my whole body and clung to him with all four limbs: legs and feet and we fell over together.

The professor said that I was very pretty, that when I grew up we'd court and he'd teach me things just as nice as drawing and painting but he wouldn't tell me any more about our plans for the moment and they were really only his plans and I assumed that they involved more and bigger exhibitions so I jumped on him again and kissed him. Then he kissed me back with a blue kiss that touched me in places I won't name because it wouldn't be decent so I went to find a big canvas and without drawing first I painted two red mouths pressing, locked, united, inseparable, singing, and a pair of eyes above, blue with fainting crystal tears. The professor kneeled down to kiss the painting and I left him still kneeling in the shadows and went home.

I told Mother about the exhibition and she who knew nothing about art answered that the shapeless nonsense I made on my cardboard would make the people who went to the School of Fine Art laugh but if the professor thought otherwise she had no objection.

When I exhibited, alongside works by other students, two of my paintings were sold. One of them was the kisses unfortunately. The professor called it *First Love*. I thought that sounded fine. But I didn't fully understand it.

Yuna is very promising, the professor said, and I loved it every time he said it and stayed after class to jump on him. He never scolded me. But when my little breasts grew he told me not to jump on him because men were fire and women straw. I didn't understand. I stopped jumping.

The Diploma

So I received a diploma in painting and drawing from the School of Fine Art when I turned seventeen but because of my lisp I couldn't teach a class or give private lessons. But I still painted when I was able to buy cardboard because the professor gave me paints when he came to visit.

Betina and her harumming chair wheeled around and around the professor until he was dizzy but Mother never left me alone with him and once slapped me because she saw us kissing but just on the cheek not the mouth like movie stars.

I was afraid that she wouldn't let the professor come in. But she did as long as we didn't go around kissing each other because if the devil stuck in his tail and the professor stuck in another part of his male anatomy I could get pregnant and the professor would never marry a handicapped student.

Betina wheeled around more than ever when the professor came to give me private classes and looked at the cardboard and canvases that were leaned up against the wall for an exhibition in Buenos Aires.

Once the class happened at night and Mother invited the teacher to dinner and he accepted. I shuddered to think about the disgusting noises, splashing, and smells that emanated from Betina's fat body. But I wasn't the captain of the ship.

Rufina had made cannelloni. It reminded me of the cannelloni at the Cottolengo. I felt an urge to paint to clear my head. I did a painting on cardboard that only I could understand. A cannelloni with eyes and a hand stretched out in a blessing. I whispered in my head: If you have a soul God will welcome you to his bosom . . .

The Dinner

Rufina took out the embroidered tablecloth that mother kept safe and the good plates which she also kept safe. When she laid the table like that my mother's eyes misted over because they were gifts from when she got engaged. They must have reminded her of when she got disengaged and father left. I never felt sorry for her because I didn't love her.

What did I care . . . Father must have found someone better who didn't have a pointer. Father probably had normal little children not freaks like hers which is to say us.

In the middle of the table stood a ceramic statuette of a pair of villagers hugging underneath a willow tree. One day I'd paint the scene which moved me because every seventeen-year-old girl wants to be hugged underneath a tree in the woods.

We ate off the special crockery because the set we used every day was chipped and stained from use. The cutlery was also the best we had and Mother kept it safe, saying it was her wedding set. The crystal came out for the first time in several years and it was like clear water. The stew dish looked completely different settled in among all that extravagance.

There was even sweet wine. Not the other kind because there wasn't enough money. There was water in the water jug and glasses, of course.

Mother sat down at the head of the table first with the professor next to her because he arrived on time and brought candy.

I sat opposite the professor and Betina was next to me.

Mother said we'd have something to peck at first. I wondered where the beak would come from and whether it was another utensil we'd never seen but that wasn't it, it was some small dishes of salami and cheese with little sword-shaped skewers.

Mother said, Help yourselves, whet your appetite, and poured wine in the grown-ups' glasses and water in Betina's and mine and when the doorbell rang in came Aunt Nené who Mother said was our surprise.

Rufina came and went looking flustered. Now she went to help Aunt Nené.

The main dish was liberated from the kitchen by Nené. It was the same chicken stew as ever but served in a silver dish and accompanied by the vegetables Nené had brought it looked fit for a king.

We each began our meal as best we could. Mother kept watch, her pointer wasn't visible but I knew she had it within reach under the table.

The most memorable and disgusting performance was given by Betina. She fumbled around, making rude noises with her bottom and burps immediately followed by Mother's apologies saying that the poor thing was sixteen but had a mental age of four according to the tests.

Aunt Nené rounded the scene off with the lamentation, How unfortunate, Clelia, which was mother's name, two idiot daughters . . . before shoving a piece of breast into her mouth, which was painted mailbox red.

The professor said that I wasn't an idiot, I was an introspective artist and I was going to hold an exhibition of paintings in Buenos Aires and I'd already sold two in the city.

Aunt Nené

Aunt Nené painted too. She had her canvases framed and hung all over the house where she lived with her mother who was my grandmother and my mother's mother. At home two paintings hung from the walls signed "Nené," faces of young women with very dark eyes, cow's eyes, and features that scared me. One had a mustache. Nené said that she liked to paint portraits and said so to the professor who asked her where she had learned the art of handling oils and such and she admitted that she was an amateur, that she didn't need anyone to hold her hand because her art poured forth from her heart like pure spring water.

The professor didn't respond to this. Nené looked at a painting I had done and said that the stripes didn't mean anything, she didn't like the new painters and she'd once laughed at

Pettoruti's cubist baloney. The teacher was standing looking at Nené's painting but now he tripped and fell on his bottom.

Aunt Nené went on to say that perhaps my nonsense meant something to me in my cognitively inhibited state . . . But who knows what the retarded think or feel, she asked aloud.

The teacher insisted that I was the best student at the School of Fine Art, that I'd graduated and would soon be exhibiting my work and Aunt Nené said sarcastically, Imagine what the others must be like, and things began to get heated.

Mother interjected that my work was a childish phase and that I'd soon get over it.

The huge eyes painted by Nené stared out at us from the wooden frame. I came out with something that would later earn me a blow from the pointer: I think a cow is looking at me and asking me if I'm going to eat it because the portrait is as boring as the face of a cow and as ugly as the face of an ugly woman.

Nené howled like a monkey at the zoo and screamed that her poor sister had put up with me for too long it was time to send me to the Cottolengo.

The professor said that he had a stomachache and asked permission to vomit in the bathroom. I was as happy as if I'd won an award for my painting.

Silence fell. Mother told Nené she'd gone too far, she should remember that I felt fulfilled making those things on the cardboard and canvas that the teacher gave me. Nené sprang up like a wasp: Can't you see that that man looks at the girl with evil intentions, she asked, but Mother told her not to think badly of others and it seemed to her that eyes so big didn't fit on the face of any woman, except perhaps the bull's wife.

I sensed that my mother accepted me and held back a tear that was about to roll down and land on the floor, the gigantic tear that I'd not been able to shed since I first began to understand—some of—what people known as normal like Mother and Nené were saying to one another. The professor came back from vomiting and addressed Nené—although she interrupted him—and what he said was:

Miss, he began, and she told him that she was a Mrs. and he apologized saying that such a pretty woman her age could never be a Miss and that her husband must be proud to have a painter by his side and she told him that they'd separated because the common ways of her ex had grated on her. The polite, learned professor couldn't help making a face that said he couldn't get anything right in this house.

Mother realized that the tarnished dinner had upset everyone apart from Nené. She brought in a tray and glasses of champagne. She'd been saving the champagne to toast the fifteenth birthday of one of her daughters meaning Betina or me but never opened it on the basis that chronological age didn't matter when hours and days had no bearing on intelligence.

We went back to the table. Betina was snoring in her high

chair. So ugly, so horrible, how was it possible that someone so ugly and horrible existed, buffalo head, dank cloth stink. Poor thing . . .

Let's toast to peace, said Nené trying to sound intellectual. And she went on to say that she felt guilty about her failed marriage because her sexual education had been lacking and sometimes she missed Sancho, which was her ex's name.

She waited for someone to ask a question but no one did so she said that on the first night, now she went red in the face, she escaped the house and garden of her enamored husband and the nuptials weren't consummated and he left. He just disappeared.

She filled her second glass of champagne and the ears of her audience with the clarification that she was a married virgin, not a Miss or a Mrs. or anything which was why she took refuge in the art of painting.

About My Aunt Nené

She spent her life clinging to the skirts of the mother who was also my mother's mother which is to say mine and Betina's grandmother. My grandmother's skirts were like a priest's cassock and her shoes were sturdy like men's shoes while her hair was tied up in a black bun because her mother was an Indian and Indians don't go gray, maybe because they don't think. Like my grandmother, Mother didn't have any gray hair but she did think.

Nené played the guitar by ear, when she played she wore a blue-and-white headband, and she hated gringos. My thoughts get away from me when I try to describe her, there are a lot of them and they're very silly but it would be fair to call her a character.

She liked to date and kiss until she swallowed her boy-friend's lips and she had about eight hundred of them but still preserved her virginity by leaping out of her wedding bed following a ceremony at the register office and a white church wedding.

Back in the early 1930s Nené fell in love with an Italian carpenter. I remember how handsome the carpenter was . . . Tall, blond, always clean and wearing cologne. He came to court her at the door of grandmother's house which wasn't worth much because it was just a little neighborhood cottage. But because no one in the family worked they had to make do with what Uncle Tito who worked for the newspapers sent them.

Aunt Nené gloried in the kisses she received. But they never did anything else because she wanted to marry in a state of virginity. I didn't understand. I thought it meant that one could protect oneself from something very sinful that I associated with pregnancy by wearing a medallion of the Virgin. Maybe when you got married you had to take off the medallion so the Virgin didn't see, who knows what it was that the Lord's mother wasn't supposed to see. I had great big messes in my head that I poured out onto my cardboard so I painted a delicate little neck from which hung a necklace with the Virgin of Luján and from out of the shadows I made by rubbing thick black lines with my finger came a big man like the Basque milkman who brought us our milk and was always calling out something like "arrauia" and from the large body fell heavy liquid that swamped the fragile neck and the Virgin wept. To show the weeping I painted red spatters of devastation that scorched the little figure on her lily neck.

The Italian boyfriend finished the bedroom, the bed and the bedside tables with fine wood. Then he made the dining room furniture and other knickknacks that every decent home needs. Aunt Nené, I know this because I listened at the door, laughed at the gringo. Does that wop think I'm going to marry him and eat pasta? Once I said to her: better pasta than just white coffee almost all the time.

She told me that I had to help her get the Italian off her back because she was now sick of him and I said I wouldn't, I wouldn't do anything bad. She said that my father who was a gringo too had left mother. I asked her if she wasn't ashamed of deceiving a good man like that and she said that wops were frauds, they weren't gentlemen, and that night she went to Chascomús where one of her brothers lived, which is to say one of my uncles and my mother's brother too.

After that I didn't hear any more about the entanglement but it was a year before Nené went back to her mother's house after which she was afraid to leave in case she met the Italian. Fortunately I heard that after his disappointment with Nené he'd engaged in nuptials with a woman from Genoa and the woman was already pregnant and I thought that she must not wear her Virgin medallion because of the contact with her husband that the Virgin mustn't see or hear.

Soon afterward Aunt Nené began seeing an Argentine boyfriend who came from Córdoba. I liked to hear his singsong accent and painted something about it.

The couple sang together and she played the guitar while a friend passed around the mate gourd. It didn't last long. This gentleman didn't build furniture or anything. One evening in June—when it gets dark early—he pressed her against a wall and she crowed like a cock at dawn and the nightwatchman on the corner came and peeled off the brazen man—he had to peel him away because he was stuck to my aunt's body—and took him down to the jail.

It was a brief and scandalous romance. I think she had others but just for looking until Don Sancho appeared and won her.

Don Sancho was a Spanish republican who I loved because he looked like Don Quixote de la Mancha.

I had a hardback book with a drawing of the Knight of Rocinante the horse and Sancho Panza but my aunt's boyfriend didn't have a belly, he was skinny as a rake and so well-spoken that I always hoped they'd come over the both of them, him and her, to drink tea and eat the cookies he'd brought. I wasn't interested in the tea and cookies, I wanted to hear Don Sancho's voice. He told stories about his adventures in his far-off homeland that gave me inspiration for my paintings and my ears savored the names of places like Paseo de la Infanta, the Manzanares River full of apples dancing in the waves like chubby-cheeked angels, which I painted.

Don Sancho gave me a fine porcelain doll that I had to call Nené, the name of my aunt and his beloved. Mother protested that I would be turning fourteen soon, I was too old for dolls. I put it on my bed and we hugged at night.

I understood that my fate loomed gloomy cloudy rainy lonely when mother shook my bedsheets, tossing Nené my doll and smashing away her charms and I came down sick with a trembling that lingered for a long time. After the smashing I grew up. Something shattered inside me hurt. Shards of porcelain Nené, my doll, stuck into my liver giving me nervous hepatitis, and I learned to cry.

I also cried when Aunt Nené left her husband, who was Don Sancho. One day I asked her why she didn't do her wifely duty. She answered that she couldn't discuss intimacies with me because as her niece I owed her respect and there'd be plenty of time later to talk about spicy, dirty things.

I told her that her sister, my other aunt, must do spicy, disgusting things with her husband and she told me to shut my mouth.

Aunt Ingrazia

My other aunt was married to Danielito, her cousin, and had two daughters. There must have been an evil eye on our family because my imbecilic younger cousins went to schools for the handicapped and one of them had six toes on each foot and a growth on her right hand that almost looked like an extra finger. But it wasn't.

The other cousin, people said, was Lilliputian, meaning a dwarf.

Aunt Ingrazia took them out of school and Carina the eldest had a boyfriend when she was fourteen and the other cousin Petra who was twelve spied on them. Uncle Danielito had a weak character and let the household drift like a rudderless boat. Ingrazia hated me because I painted and was pretty like one of Modigliani's models, in *The Girl in the Tie*.

Aunt Ingrazia said that I was handicapped too but I hid my abnormality by painting and being pretty. I think she was right . . . I lived only to sit down and paint and the world around me faded into a lovely island of different shades.

Aunt Ingrazia lived on the outskirts of the city in a big house surrounded by a garden. Uncle Danielito worked in a notary's office and wasn't at the family home very much.

I grew up with a shallow opinion of the concept of marriage and a stable family. I swore I would never get married. I swore I would live to paint. I swore a lot of things until I found out that swearing was a sin and never swore again.

When Carina got pregnant, Aunt Nené came over very upset and told Aunt Ingrazia they should get an abortion. A fifteen-year-old single mother, no, never . . .

I asked Petra if she had seen how a boy gets a girl pregnant and she said that I was retarded even if I did paint and she'd never known anyone as ignorant as I was and she told me everything.

At the age of eighteen a fourteen-year-old girl opened my eyes. It made me sad, like the abortion which I dreamed and painted. I painted a map of the world on a big piece of cardboard with a tadpole floating inside it, striving to protect itself from a trident that was trying to skewer it and suddenly the tadpole looked like a human seed, an ugly boy that grew cuter every minute until it was a baby and then the trident pierced him in his little belly and he floated outside the map of the world. The painting depicted several different stages of the little creature's adventure and was studied with great interest and also used by social psychologists to ask me questions that I answered as best I could to throw them off track. I think I did. I read the childish conclusions they came to. Privately I made fun of them, their posturing and their pity for me.

When I gave the work a title, I think they realized their mistake: *Abortion*. That was my title.

I won a medal for *Abortion*.

Aunt Nené and My Cousin Carina

Carina begged me to stay with her all day and right through the night until the next morning because she was afraid.

I stayed. I confess that her stupidity and six toes disgusted me.

She told me that when she was in the kitchen of the big house, which was how I already described, big and roomy, the neighbor from the house next door came over and they started to kiss, "He kissed me so much . . ." and then they got half naked and he pushed against her and she didn't understand why her privates hurt the first time and it bled a lot but she didn't tell her mother, which is to say Aunt Ingrazia. Now she knew that she should have told her because Aunt Nené screamed, You pregnant retard, and was going to take her somewhere to get rid of the pregnancy and also she asked me for advice. But I didn't say anything because I didn't yet know where I stood on the issue. She hugged me.

When Nené arrived at eleven the next day we were ready and we went off with her in one of those covered cabs pulled by a horse to the edge of the city center. We got out in a poor neighborhood. *Hellish* would be the title of my next work, which I already had inside me like Carina, as I now know, had the baby inside her but Nené said that it wasn't yet a baby only three months after the original sin committed by my cousin Carina and the man from the farm next door, the flower grower who was old and married and could easily have been the disgraced Carina's father and we weren't to say anything to anyone, not even Uncle Danielito who was her cousin and also mother's and Aunt Ingrazia's. She added that Danielito was a fool but there was a chance he might get angry and we'd suffer a family tragedy along with this filthy business.

I noticed that Carina was sobbing without shedding any tears and stroked her belly with her fingers when Aunt Nené said filthy business and realized that Carina wanted the baby she had inside her and I got goose bumps.

We walked through the poor neighborhood and out of the poorest house came an old woman in a robe and apron drying her hands, inviting us in, the doctor was on her way. We sat down to wait on a sofa that billowed dust because it hadn't been beaten and I sneezed because I'm allergic.

In the mirror hanging from the wall opposite I saw how insignificant we were, Aunt Nené too with her suit that fit too tight because she was fat and the open toe shoes with the painted nails and the face that looked like the cow faces she painted (you aren't going to eat me, I said to myself). But now a weak voice was asking why are you going to kill me, only I heard it in a different way—just me.

I heard people walking around in the next room getting the equipment ready, I knew it because the metallic noises were like the ones I heard when I had my tonsils taken out at the Hospital Italiano.

The doctor came but she didn't look like one she looked common. She asked who the patient was and how many months and Aunt Nené answered three-and-change and I understood why people say that children bring good luck but Aunt Nené who didn't eat every day for lack of money wouldn't pardon the baby even with the change it brought.

Come in, said the doctor, and Carina went inside trembling, she asked if her aunt could come too and the doctor said no and closed the door to the other room.

The metallic screech of the equipment grew more shrill. Carina didn't cry. I realized that there was someone else there in addition to the doctor. An hour and a half later the door opened and the doctor said we could come in. Carina was still on the table, sleeping from the anesthesia. The doctor called Aunt Nené over and I heard her say forty pesos. What a racket . . . Nené exclaimed.

I took hold of Carina's ugly hand. She squeezed mine and I was glad she wasn't dead.

When she had recovered they called a car. And we went back to Aunt Ingrazia and Carina's house. Nené didn't get out and went home in the same car. Beforehand she whispered to us not to say anything about it to anyone because abortions were forbidden by law and if it got out we'd all be sent to Olmos Prison.

Petra

Carina's sister, Petra, another of my cousins, came out to meet Carina and me. She wanted details and we made her swear that she wouldn't tell or we'd end up in Olmos Prison. You would, the dwarf screamed, because I didn't go, and I warned her that if she blabbed what Carina told her in her innocence, I'd accuse her of forcing Carina to get the abortion. She swore not to tell.

Also she promised to teach us how women didn't get pregnant if they took precautions (the methods). I asked her how she knew so much if she was just fourteen. She told me she'd been doing it since she was twelve. But after her menstruation she used condoms or counted a certain number of days—I don't remember how many—when she could do without one. But she said it was best not to trust the calendar.

Carina went off to her little bed and asked for milky tea and toast.

Petra said that there was no reason to deprive yourself of anything and using a condom was good but it had to be put on properly because if not it could break and then . . .

I asked where you had to put the condom, in your handbag, or pocket, or . . .

Petra opened her hippopotamus mouth and told me where and how. I had to vomit what I hadn't eaten and walked home to get some air and see if I couldn't forget the particulars of the adventure I'd got involved in out of pity for Carina. Now I was upset about a dead baby who couldn't defend himself. But I consoled myself remembering that Nené had said that at three-months-and-change it wasn't anyone or anything.

The Warm Embrace of Home

Aunt Nené said that she missed the warm embrace of the cottage where she lived with her old mother who was also the mother of my mother and Aunt Ingrazia and grandmother to all of us and that in that hallowed place she was happy because she loved her mother and when they got money from her brother—I shan't go through all the ties—they bought cookies and candy and red and white wine and the two of them feasted talking about old times and she wouldn't know what to do with herself without her mother.

I told her that Grandma was so old that she was going to die any day now and she slapped me. Then I hissed into Nené's ear that she'd organized the crime against Carina's baby and the guardian angels of children would punish her for it. The offended woman screeched that my mother would hear about how I'd disrespected her and my mother would send me to bed without dessert, the one I liked, peaches in syrup. She left.

At home about an hour later, the telephone rang. It was Nené tearfully saying that Grandma was lying stiff in bed which is to say dead.

We all went, even Betina in her wheelchair. We found Aunt Nené sitting with our grandmother on her lap on the sofa in the drawing room sobbing Mama is mine . . . Mama is mine . . . Mama is mine . . .

Grandma's two sons came, Nené and mother's brothers, also Ingrazia and Danielito you already know and between them they couldn't pry Grandma from Aunt Nené's arms.

One pulled to the north, the other to the south, the other to the east, and the last to the west. I shouted that they were going to break her like my doll Nené who Don Sancho, Nené's husband, had given to me and the filial bonds were relaxed and because Grandma was stiff, absolutely stiff they put her in bed and had great difficulty closing her eyes because her eyelids were like dried leaves. It was quite unpleasant to see that she could no longer see us but the dead have nothing to look at and they said they'd call the funeral home to have her put in a coffin which made Aunt Nené howl: Mama is mine I won't let you shut her away or bury her . . .

So they called a nurse who gave her sedative and our aunt

fell asleep on the sofa with her mouth open from which two false teeth slipped out and I picked them up and flushed them down the toilet.

It was my revenge for Carina's tears. I enjoyed watching the preparations for the funeral and Grandma being put into the coffin. She'd been dressed in a shroud and looked like a very old woman. Neighbors came by and some relatives I didn't know.

Betina was hidden in the attic with the other useless things to avoid problems with poo and pee.

The little house was full and guests were served coffee in small cups. Not many people look sad at wakes because they talk and laugh, drink coffee and if there's something to nibble on the occasion doesn't put them off.

While this was going on Aunt Nené woke up and howling like a wolf screamed the same things as before rudely pushing the relatives and friends away from the deceased grandma, She's mine, mine . . .

She demanded they give the body to her to take to the bedroom because it was time for her tea. When she touched her she screamed that they'd let her freeze, she was cold, so cold. Then she shouted that she'd lost her teeth and she stopped crying about Grandma and cried over her teeth because they had gold in them.

She went to the kitchen and brought back a bed warmer with hot coals to warm up her mother, my grandma, and put it under the coffin because no one dared to challenge behavior that was only making the tragicomedy worse. When I think, I use elegant, learned words that don't come to me in speech.

It was a few hours before it would be time to take the deceased to the cemetery and bury her but the heat from the warmer started to puff Grandma up gradually meaning she wasn't skinny anymore, she was looking quite well and rosy although she gave off an unpleasant odor. A gentleman from the funeral home said to take the warmer away because the heat was accelerating the putrefaction and Aunt Nené hit the man who quickly disappeared from the scene replaced by buzzing flies that headed straight for the sleeping body and Aunt Nené shooed them away with a Spanish fan given to her by Don Sancho who was the only absent relative. I don't know if he's a relative or not. He didn't come. It was for the best.

The smell was now spreading and many were offering their condolences and leaving while Aunt Nené fought a ferocious fan battle with flies dressed in greenish blue singing their gluttonous tunes.

Aunt Nené's big black cow eyes looked out at the few guests still left and Grandma got fatter. Aunt Nené said, See how much better she is? The nurse gave her a sedative and Aunt Nené fell back into the stupor allowing the undertakers to put the coffin lid over Grandma and spray fly killer to improve the atmosphere.

When Aunt Nené came around, she wanted to see her mother but she'd been shut in already and so she threw herself to the floor and banged her head against the floorboards, repeating her demand. A priest interceded, saying that such a true daughter deserved to have her wish granted. They slid the lid back a little and Aunt Nené screamed that she'd been switched, this wasn't the face of her beloved mother, it was a frog. The nurse put her back to sleep.

When the time came to take the frog-grandma to the cemetery, Aunt Nené went into the back of the house and said: Mama, they've taken the frog away, you can come out now.

Impatiens

Aunt Nené stayed on at the little house but said that she was making dinner for herself and her mother and everyone realized that a screw had come loose, saying that someone should stay with her until she got better because a healthy woman like Nené ought to recover from the shock to the psyche that comes with the enormous pain over the death of a mother. Just then the professor appeared apologizing for not coming sooner to offer his condolences. He said that although he had no blood ties, he was willing to take care of the grief-stricken woman and make her dinner and perhaps someone else should stay with him because friends must stick together during difficult times.

Danielito offered to pay the nurse who agreed and I offered to keep everyone company.

While Aunt Nené shuffled between the kitchen and the dining room laying the table, and put potatoes, yams, and eggs on to boil and also some other vegetables and a little meat left over from their last stew, I set up two cardboards—I always carried cardboard with me—and felt inspiration come to me in hurried brushstrokes of images depicting the different events of the rich, full, Goyaesque week. As I said, inside my psyche I was familiar with nuances and shapes quite different from the fool I was on the outside who spoke without periods or commas because if she added a period or comma she'd lose her speech entirely. Sometimes I added a period or comma just to take a breath but it was better to talk out loud quickly so people could understand me and avoid long silent gaps that revealed my difficulties with verbal communication because when I heard myself I got confused between the noises inside my head and the sibilant flow of words and I gaped at how there were fat words and skinny words, black and white words, crazy and insightful words, and words that slept in dictionaries that no one used. Here, for example, I have used commas. And periods. But now I must go out to the garden to take a breath and talk to myself in the garden where plants grow in beds full of red flowers, so, so, so many called impatiens and one afternoon I wanted to cut a stalk to put in the vase in the dining room in Grandma's house which now belonged to Aunt Nené and they told me that they didn't like them because they were wild and not for indoors and Aunt Nené tipped them out of the vase with the water and all leaving the vase empty on the table.

And because I felt like livening up the black, bare, oval table I filled the vase with pump water and cut plenty of impatiens to treat myself.

The professor helped Aunt Nené to peel potatoes and yams and wash the vegetables and went to buy an oxtail bone to add flavor. I wasn't hungry.

We sat at the table: the teacher, the nurse, me, and Aunt Nené who came and went serving the food. I saw that she set a plate for Grandma but Grandma wasn't there.

She said, Mama would you like a little more, and answered herself, Certainly my dear, which scared me because it was in Grandma's voice even though Grandma was buried in the ground and had blown up like a balloon thanks to the heat from the warmer that Aunt Nené had put underneath the coffin.

The professor and the nurse looked at each other, shaking their heads with pitying concern and sighing because my aunt had gone mad or had acquired the ability to see things we couldn't. It's said that some people can see the dead who are called spiritualists.

Every time Nené went to the kitchen to get something the nurse moved a potato, yam, and boiled egg from Grandma's plate to hers, emptying it as though a diner had been hungrily eating which made Nené exclaim that it was the first time Mama had ever eaten on her own without her having to help. And she said that she looked chubbier and rosier and the lipstick and big, almost open-mouthed smile on her face brought back some of the youth she'd lost during a hardworking life as a widow caring for children and witnessing her failed marriage to the Spaniard Sancho who gave me the doll that Mother broke because she'd told her to break it because she thought the Spaniard was looking at my titties when I was developed.

I was so angry that I almost told her that Grandma's chair was empty and that Grandma was rotting under the ground and the worms would feast on her body like the worms in the story that sucked on Mr. Valdemar's face, but I held these facts back for later.

Addressing myself to the professor I reminded him of the story and the professor went red as a tomato waggling his finger at me to be quiet and adding that he couldn't remember the story and even if he could it had nothing to do with anything, but the circumstances of Nené's destruction and the slander that Don Sancho had dirty inclinations toward me set me against Aunt Nené and even more so against Mother who believed her and it broke my heart just like Doll-Nené's porcelain head.

I noticed that Nené drank a bottle of white wine on her own and then she sang and played the guitar and I remember well what she sang:

My dogs have died,
the farm is bereft,
now I too shall die,
so nothing is left.

The nurse dried a tear with her napkin, got up from the table and went to do the dishes and while she was doing that she remembered that Betina was still in the attic. She went up with a plate of leftovers and a piece of bread and then brought down the handicapped girl who asked what happened. Carina told her that her Grandma was in the cemetery and Aunt Nené said that she'd gone to bring flowers to who knows who.

The professor said that it was time to go and brought me my coat and cardboard. By now, it was the professor and I, Betina in her wheelchair and someone else but I forget who and the nurse who stayed behind with Aunt Nené. Aunt Nené said that Grandma was tucked up and warm in bed and that she'd do likewise.

The people I mentioned went out onto the street, Mother

and Aunt Ingrazia came saying that maybe they should stay to keep Nené company because she was surely out of her mind but then they decided that if they gave the nurse a tip they'd have done their duty and they had enough burdens without having to deal with another fat one by which I sensed they meant Aunt Nené.

I need to take a breath and so will insert a periodical parenthesis but I hasten to add that at the end of the procession of mourners was Petra pushing Betina's wheelchair, Betina was asleep, resting her head on her big breasts which weren't like my little ones, snoring. I don't know whether I've forgotten anyone. We took a covered cab pulled by a golden sorrel and I felt that to shake off all these bad feelings I'd paint a little golden animal that I'd call Pegasus even though Pegasus flapped a pair of wings from his smooth flanks.

We arrived and those still awake with me were Danielito, Petra, and Betina who asked for more food and was brought roulade and soup, Carina who didn't go to the funeral because she had a slight fever, and the professor who didn't go home to bed but stayed at the house to accompany us in our grief.

I should also say that we were at Aunt Ingrazia's house and I saw that Carina was looking poorly because of her fever, it was very noticeable and she mumbled an apology and went off to bed.

Mother drew my attention to the time and suggested we go

home and the professor agreed that it was no time for one to still be on their feet and when he went to pick up the hat he'd left on a chair Mother stopped him with an I don't mean you, professor. Betina opened her eyes wide and said she didn't want to go and Petra said that she could sleep in the kitchen, warmed by the embers from the stove in the recliner that Carina had been in just a little while before. Mother, the professor, and I went back home in the cab that was waiting for us in the street.

The professor expressed his concern over the absence of my sister who was sitting in the orthopedic chair at Aunt Ingrazia's house, Mother said she was worried about Carina's fever and she had plenty of reason to believe that the child who was deformed on the outside had a kind heart in her breast and if her arms weren't so short she'd paint better than I did with my blurry nonsense on cardboard that no one understood. And she added ironically that God gives bread to the toothless, giving me a disapproving look.

The professor put cardboard on the wall and told me to paint something as golden as the sun because all that gloom and sorrow breaks your soul and I felt that the professor was referring to the inner sheet but to break it would have to be starched or I don't know what, I don't know how something that brings life to one's somatic, a word I copied from the dictionary, self can break.

Pegasus looked lovely trotting along a golden river whose

shores shone with sunflowers from Holland and some black
birds broke up the golden landscape because one always needs
something ugly in a scene as golden as it might be.

The professor left in the autumn drizzle. I fell asleep on
the sofa as though I were waiting for something even though I
didn't know what it was but it happened the telephone rang and
Petra's voice reported that Carina had vomited and her fever
was soaring and Aunt Ingrazia was waiting for morning to call
a doctor.

When I looked at Pegasus I saw that Carina was riding on
his beautiful croup and whispered the question where are you
going and they answered they were going to see the man in the
moon and I knew that there was no point calling a doctor for
Carina because she had gone to look for her lost baby. I slept
calmly until the next day when I was informed of Carina's sud-
den death which I already knew about and I was happy because
she was better off anywhere other than this sorry world.

More family mourning. When Aunt Nené heard that
Carina no longer belonged to this dark universe she was struck
by the horrible memory of a journey to a dirty neighborhood,
a visit to a nasty hovel, an operation called an abortion and she
put it all together. But she shut her mouth, which was missing
the false teeth I'd flushed down the toilet and was afraid that I'd
say something that might compromise her and came over to me
during the wake to hiss that I was involved too and didn't have

any evidence and I ran away from her the way you do from a poisonous bug or a scorpion.

This new incident drove Nené's mother's funeral from her mind, and during the ceremony she kept her cow eyes on me. I stuck my tongue out at her.

When they picked up the little box where Carina would rest forever I saw that it barely weighed anything and said to myself that she had flown off on her horse to where unbaptized babies go which is called limbo so the father from catechism told me when I took my first communion and I prayed an Our Father adding words for the angels telling them to let Carina and her little unbaptized child float up to a gentle part of Purgatory because it had been killed before it was born. When it came to Carina, I asked the Virgin of Luján to forgive her even though I didn't know for what or why or how a baby could have got into her belly or what role the man from around the corner had played with her in the kitchen and I told the Virgin that it was a nightmare and that she who had been a mother knew well that all you needed was a ray of light brought by a holy spirit dove to get a developed young lady pregnant and if she hadn't been developed nothing would have happened and Carina would still be with us good and quiet like she always was.

We put her in a grave nearby Grandma's grave which Aunt

Nené either didn't or pretended not to see and I started to suspect her and everyone except my little sister Betina with the severe handicap.

When flowers get angry they waggle their pistils and wrinkle their petals which look like slippery poisonous creatures their appearance changes they're not fully vegetable or animal more like evil gnomes or nymphs and not because they want to be but because certain human behaviors make them disgusted and angry and they already suffer enough when they're picked and taken to the florists without realizing that their pollen when the wind blows and the pollen falls on fertile ground little plants are born like the plants that gave them their grace and color. But when they're pulled out often not even the water in the vases will help them and they get ashamed of the bad smell they give off especially at funeral homes which along with the deceased represent an insult to beauty and creation.

The flowers in the beds of what was now Aunt Nené's house which was Grandma's before but not anymore because she was dead hated Aunt Nené because they'd heard her scorn them and reject their offspring from her table because they were weeds and shout, Get that rubbish out of here, and when Uncle Sancho who never consummated his marriage with her but who was her husband brought her red and white roses she did like those and please let me interject that I don't understand what not consummating the marriage means and I'm going to ask Petra who knows a lot about such chicanery, a word I heard someone say once I don't know who but it's nice so I use it.

We went back into Aunt Ingrazia's house to begin the wake.

I took my cardboard and Aunt Nené called me a bum and panhandler but the professor who was there too defended me and reminded her that my cardboards and canvases were being discussed in art journals and that an exhibition would soon be held in Buenos Aires not just of cardboards but canvases too open to a select public and in all her years she'd never made painting a priority and the paintings he'd seen in Grandma's house weren't worth half a bean.

Oh Mama . . . oh Mama . . . oh Mama, howled the cow-eyed monkey.

Now Aunt Ingrazia was crying on Danielito her cousin and husband's shoulder over the death of Carina and while she was at it the death of her mother, Danielito's aunt which is to say my grandmother.

I envied the fact that Carina was at peace and on cardboard I painted a faint pietà drawing on a hazy memory of the one by Michelangelo that the professor showed us at the School of Fine Art, analyzing it with such sensitivity that I had to excuse myself and leave because my chest was purring like an affectionate cat from the emotion and stayed out there until my chest had calmed down because I can't remember if I ever said that the consolation of tears was denied to me and in my chest I had a liquid lake that the doctor diagnosed as a chronic cold and when I told Mother she called the diagnosis stupid and said that I made things up to attract attention because I was vain. And the cruel word grated on my soul as though I'd been hit by a cobblestone launched from a slingshot, these being words I took from the dictionary but afterward I feel exhausted and get a migraine, another word I got from the dictionary when I looked up *headache*.

The professor and Danielito went to serve the coffee for the wake with sweet cookies and little glasses of port.

I wanted to go back home and the professor went to fetch the cab we always used and Mother declared that we all deserved a good rest and so we went back while Petra decided, to a degree, to take the place of Carina in Aunt Ingrazia and Danielito's mournful house.

I had told her that it was her duty because she was just as much the daughter of the couple as Carina was and I still had a sister, Betina, and she said that I had half a sister and the heated atmosphere after Aunt Nené's disagreement with the professor needed to cool down and although Mother said more words of condolence we all left with our tails between our legs except for Betina who dragged her soul tail along behind her and it was growing ever more elongated, a word I took from the dictionary. My vocabulary was growing richer every day although I could never be lucid because my speech turned imbecilic the moment it left my mouth.

So Aunt Nené went home walking and although she looked at the cab several times we didn't invite her in. She whispered something from her gappy mouth which as I've said was that way because I threw her false teeth into the toilet in circumstances that I shan't repeat so as not to bore those who might happen to read me and I repeat to those who do happen to read me patience because I can hear myself and if my written words sound as exhaustingly stupid as the ones I say inside anyone who finishes this absurd dirge will curse me for the time I wasted while being forced to admit that they couldn't put me down because they found among my stupid disappointments in love and death much of what they have experienced himself or herself if the reader is a lady.

When Nené got home to her mother or the deceased's house which was now hers she called on the telephone and Mother said that the call didn't smell good although I didn't smell one of Betina's farts she wasn't there so I'll never know what it was that Mother smelled when she said what she said but I worked it out the next day when the milkman came calling out his arrauia . . . Poor lady . . . and the poor lady was Aunt Nené who'd slipped in the deceased's now her garden, cracking her skull

and the funny part and here I laugh even if it's a sin at the absurdity (from the dictionary) the absurdity being that Aunt Nené
slipped on a flower that the wind blew onto her patio tiles whose
name is impatiens.

Part Two

The Neighbor

Petra had stayed in the kitchen at Aunt Ingrazia's house. When I asked her why she winked and I knew she was plotting something. When I added the period my head started to buzz so I'm going to go outside for a moment to catch my breath, I'll be back soon.

I have returned and will remind the reader that Petra is or was the sister of Carina and that Carina allowed the neighbor to put a baby in her belly. But I'm not sure on the details although I do know that it happened in the kitchen and I connected Petra's wink and decision to take her place and leave the lamp on for the neighbor to see the light and know that the way was clear like Carina said when she went red as a tomato and whispered, He kisses me so much . . .

And it's best that I tell you right now that at four in the morning Petra jumped out from the bush of hemlock and signaled to me to be quiet with her finger over her lips and we locked ourselves in my bedroom and I offered to help ameliorate (a word from the dictionary) any problem she might be having but she had to tell me about the baby you already know about. On that period I'll take a rest.

And she told me that poor Carina was hurt badly because the old married neighbor ruined her privates and made her bleed just like when her period came and then it didn't come and she knew about the pregnancy when Aunt Nené who is now accounting for her actions before the Almighty decided that we'd have to go empty her belly of the baby to preserve the family honor. I shan't repeat the rest but I think that the Almighty will cast Aunt Nené down below because you should never do such things especially not with someone little and defenseless and Petra said that she'd get her revenge for Carina and the baby and I asked how and she said that the neighbor saw the lamp and in a single leap was in the kitchen and she said she specialized in oralsess and began, although she vomited and he promised her a ring if she continued with the oralsess and so she agreed. I diligently looked up the meaning of *oralsess* in the dictionary but for the first time my research met a dead end, so I had no choice but to ask Petra what oralsess meant in person.

But now I've written both a period and a comma and my head is going buzzbuzzbuzz and I'm going out to get some air but I'll be back before Petra appears her features have changed on account of her rage over the injustices that were committed against Carina and the poor baby and I don't understand how the baby got into my cousin's belly but I told Petra that I did understand and she earnestly told me that she'd fix all this mess of injustice with her oralsess that taunted me so which the gentlemen who make dictionaries appear to have forgotten or else it's a new term because there are a lot of new terms these days.

I go back to my cardboard and paint my feelings doubts and strange speculations regarding life, destiny, and death and come to awful conclusions because while Aunt Nené dying made sense, the death of Carina's baby didn't and neither did that of Carina who didn't do anything wrong and if you don't believe me look at all the little images of the Virgin you see packing the churches and homes where the beautiful lady is lovingly cradling the little child and there's nothing repulsive about that and although that child was killed it was when he was thirty-three and religion says that his death was unjust too but that young man was going to come back to life not like Carina's baby who I'd have liked to cradle.

I'm exhausted by all the punctuation and commas you need to breathe otherwise I'd suffocate and I don't want to go until I've shown a significant number of paintings in the gallery of the School of Fine Art, the professor said that it would be a solo show meaning just one person that person being the author of these living documents that someone will read and be amazed not at the writing which lacks Literary Style but the paintings they refer to and it will be covered in newspapers and magazines and I'm proud of my work and the fact that the professor calls me the girl in the tie because of my resemblance to Modigliani's melancholy young woman. Everything that has happened goes into my pictures it being the story of a strange family but sometimes I think that all families have something strange about them but they hide it for example Amalia is a classmate at the School of Fine Art and she told me that to save her family from starving and to give herself the luxury of studying she had to sleep with a rich man who would give her money every time he slept with her and she would give it to her mother and there would also be enough to study. And that the first time the man realized that she was chaste and asked why she'd deceived him saying she wasn't and she already naked in bed said that it was because she was hungry and wanted to study and the man didn't do anything to her and told her to get dressed and then he gave her a job and never saw her again and that only many years later did she arrive at the conclusion that the gentleman was the best she'd ever known because later she slept with others and I didn't see anything wrong with that until she told me about it in great detail. I never saw Amalia again.

Meanwhile Mother still taught, but there was a change that took me by surprise when the professor suggested to Mother that she take him in as a lodger at home so he could help take care of Betina and Yuna, who is me in case you've forgotten, and she could rest easy because he was a forty-year-old bachelor of unimpeachable conduct and he could also help Rufina in the kitchen. Petra who always knew about everything said how good it would be if the professor were in love with my mother not because she liked the professor but because my father even though he forgot about us lived somewhere and Mother was a teacher and should be an example to the children and not give anyone anything to gossip about and I asked the professor about it and he laughed saying he'd never heard anything so crazy, Mother was a decent married woman. And I was reassured.

I need to rest.

I haven't dedicated much space to the mass and other ceremonies held for Aunt Nené's passing. I didn't feel anything.

Another rest.

I'll have to a leave out the periods or else I'll never finish this screed.

The professor moved into the attic and climbed up a wooden staircase that creaked with age and damp and with the help of the movers carried up his bed wardrobe a little table and lots of packages and piles of books and I didn't like having him so close by because it meant the trip to the School of Fine Art wasn't so exciting although now he went with me and everyone thought he was my father or an older boyfriend the idiots they couldn't conceive of a friendship for friendship's sake and that nothing else was going on between the professor and me and I swear that it's the pure truth on Carina's soul I swear crossing my fingers may the Lord punish me if I lie.

Oh . . . oh . . . oh. I take a deep breath and announce my exhibition of thirty cardboards and ten canvases and admit that I was terrified by the flashes from the cameras and the professor's eagerness to read the newspapers the next day in which they said that I was worth my weight in gold but I was so skinny I weighed barely ninety pounds and I said so and everyone said that in addition to being a brilliant painter I was witty and very sociable.

After the event my life changed because requests were made for illustrations for books and magazines and they also requested my presence on the TV and the radio to ask me who knows what because I never went because I was scared the professor said that I was very shy but that very talented painters are rare so I shouldn't worry and should keep doing what I was doing he was my representative and would arrange things with the print press and television.

And as it happened enormous inspiration came to me and

I dreamed the events I'd experienced transforming them into figures ever more colorful and beautiful that in my imagination moved and talked to me forcing me to take them outside of me and pour them onto the cardboard and canvases and I was kind of a strange creature subject to the whims of these tyrannical shapes and figures and if I didn't answer they'd bite my brain with glass teeth and my heart when the experience meant something and bully their way out onto the canvas or cardboard. I feel bad when I don't do my duty to the whispering voices that harass me and congratulate myself when once I've finished the painting I am applauded quietly by invisible hands like butter-fly wings and hear the chirping of tiny little ineffable birds like hummingbirds singing praises and I know that the work is good enough to be entered for a prize or exhibition.

I was surprised that no one at home acknowledged the changes brought about by what I'd been doing or the money I contributed which wasn't a small amount because it allowed them to build a terrace and another bedroom and buy new furniture.

I dressed elegantly, my feminine sensibility dictated the cut of suits, dresses, and shoes etc. that were right for me and I read about the lives of painters who I was becoming like without meaning to and that made me happy because I knew that paint-ing was a vocation and not just the whim of a stuck-up girl like my mother had said some time ago and she didn't say it anymore but I still refused to forgive her. I came to the conclusion that I must earn more than her, she was just a plain old teacher. I'll take a rest and go out to enjoy the air of the aurora borealis.

The Oralsess Enigma

The professor is my legal representative.

Petra who always thinks the worst of people told me to be careful with representatives who can make off with money, bonds, and such belonging to those who trusted them and she was sorry that she wasn't a legal adult so she could be my legal representative because her hands were clean and I was surprised by that because I'd never noticed that the professor's were dirty but I didn't say anything remembering my now deceased grandma's advice that there were no flies in a closed mouth and although I don't fully understand the saying I intuited (from the dictionary) that it applied to talking to my cousin Petra.

Oh . . . the periods . . . they're tiring and in my head they introduce so many ideas that they stumble over one another and then I can't remember which one I was trying to explain but on seeing Petra I get an idea and it turns out that it's that I need to ask her about oralsess because I can't find it in the dictionary.

Let me rest. Ah . . .

When I asked Petra about the term she laughed out loud and called me an idiot saying I was over eighteen but I didn't even know how to speak and posing like a sixth-grade teacher she pronounced "oral sex" which left me openmouthed but I still wanted to know more so I begged her to explain because it must be what Petra said every girl does and she sat on a chair and said pretend I'm a man, in this case that old farmer who got Carina pregnant and sitting down she opened her legs and said think that if I were a man I'd have a penis instead of my privates and *penis* means weenie which boys pee from instead of where we women do and if you don't want to get pregnant you can't let the penis enter your privates because the semen that is expelled from the penis is what contaminates them and then comes the worst part the pregnancy and that she suggested oral sex to the farmer and he gladly agreed. I'm so tired . . .

She continued her explanation still sitting with her legs open and said that oral sex means that the man puts his thing in the woman's mouth and she sucks it like it were fruit or candy and suddenly semen comes out and it doesn't get you pregnant like that. I vomited and she got angry and rightly said that she was never going to explain private things to me again although it would be good for me to know so that I can avoid what happened to innocent Carina and her baby and any man looking to stay out of trouble agrees to oral sex and she thinks they're such pigs that they like it better than the normal way and married men ask for it because they have their children with the wives they married at the register office and the church and that she who was two years younger than me earned her money with the practice and no one knew and she trusted me not to tell because she'd opened my eyes so no one would put their penis into my privates and then I'd die from an infection like Carina and the baby. I apologized for vomiting and thanked her for the class on oral sex which was very useful but said that I'd never practice it because of my delicate stomach and my liver which had suffered from hepatitis and wasn't very hardy (from the dictionary) so it could send me to hospital.

And in the hospital I'd die of shame having to tell the doctors about the cause of my difficulties. I'd never do such things, after all, I earned good money with my paintings and the illustrations I was asked for by newspapers and magazines and even if I didn't I'd prefer to work for hours like Filomena's mother and Filomena too who were poor but decent neighbors and Petra pulled my hair when I said that the two Filomenas were decent because she realized what that meant I thought of her and I apologized again, please forgive me, and she did.

Petra's Decision

Petra was the daughter of Aunt Ingrazia and sister of Carina and even though Carina was deceased she still was and she decided to sleep in the kitchen telling Aunt Ingrazia that she felt warm there because the stove was kept burning all night and Aunt Ingrazia allowed it, now she let Petra do anything because she was the only daughter she had left although her husband which is to say her cousin Danielito slept with her in the big bedroom and the matrimonial bed watched over by a painting of the Heart of Jesus that stared down at them from the wall and which Aunt Ingrazia covered with a cloth every time they behaved like a couple in love. I won't say what because the periods and commas exhaust me and I'll look ridiculous and even those good readers who have sympathy for me will stop reading.

I can't remember if I wrote that Petra was Lilliputian in stature which is what the doctors said when she was born, she fit in the palm of your hand and the godmother went into the church carrying her like an offering, all the family said so and they didn't think she was going to live but they were wrong because she was now grown and knew a lot more about life than me even though I was about to turn nineteen.

She came up to my waist because I'm tall, about five foot six and skinny, and she's chubby, her face looks like a succulent apple. She told me that at first the farmer neighbor came once a week at night, jumping over the low wall, but she'd got him so excited with her game of oral sex that now he came every other day or rather night and sometimes he came every day and earlier and earlier and she had suggested, to avoid arousing suspicion in the neighborhood because at the store they'd asked who it was who jumped over the wall and she didn't know what to say and again she suggested varying the visits meaning that he'd come one time and the next she'd go because she couldn't jump but she could climb and they'd meet in the barn where he kept his potatoes and other vegetables and greens and also fruit and flowers and he agreed but said they should keep the same routine for a week longer and she agreed.

I don't know why but a shadow of doubt that I later painted on cardboard distorted (dictionary) the atmosphere and I asked Petra what she was planning because between one subject and another she who was very talkative left gaps and she laughed in such a way that the succulent apple meaning her chubby face looked like a ball of fire and it scared me and she saw and told me that the neighbor had said that if he weren't married he'd marry her and I got even more scared because I thought they'd kill the man's wife and she read my thoughts and said that it was possible but not likely she wanted to avoid trouble with the authorities but she'd do something.

I advised her not to hurt anyone innocent and she answered that Carina was innocent and I took her arm and repeated, Don't kill the wife she's got enough problems with that stupid husband, and she screamed to let her go because I was hurting her little arm which made me think that given her lack of strength she'd find it difficult to get rid of the Italian wife who was as big as four sacks of potatoes all piled on top of one another.

I'll leave Petra and her hateful partner for a moment and watch the professor climbing the attic stairs with some books. The professor helps a lot around the house and Mother is fatter and Rufina too and I've noticed that the professor doesn't pay me so much attention because really I don't need it I can get from the house to the School of Fine Art on my own and I take private classes with a lady who was a painter and singer whose name is Doña Lola and is so well bred that she uses two surnames Juliánez Islas. She's a teacher at the school nearby whose name is Miss Mary O'Graham which is where

distinguished young ladies like Doña Lola go and the prin-
cipal offered me the events hall for an exhibition because the
professor also teaches there and the professor advised me not
to speak during the event, he'd write a page for me and I'd
read it out after practicing but they only had to see the quality
of my paintings for them to adore me and invite me to join
the group of young ladies but I shouldn't accept because I was
different and then the reputation of the work, the artist, and
her representative might be tarnished. I asked if I would be a
freak in the eyes of the ladies and gentlemen and he said he
wouldn't go so far but it was best to keep up appearances.

I went to pick out an outfit at Gath y Chaves in a bird's-eye
pattern with a velvet collar. I bought tights, buckled shoes, and
a portfolio in a leather goods store, the very best leather where
I would keep my smaller cardboard because the canvases and
bigger cardboard would be taken by the professor.

My enthusiasm and the punctuation I shan't name again
have tired me so much that I need to rest. I'll continue later.

When the Exhibition Was Held

When the paintings were hung in the enormous hall the most
important were fitted with a little light to make them stand out
and I saw that almost all my paintings were lit up and signed
Yuna Riglos but Riglos was something the professor made up
because my father's surname is López and when an older lady
read Riglos I think she forgot all about what was in the painting and came over to ask whether I was related to the Riglos
from . . . I can't remember where and I told her that my name
was Yuna López and the Riglos was on account of the professor and the lady said Ah . . . and walked off to look at another
painting and some time later I saw her leave and thought that
she wouldn't be back and then the professor came over to tell
me that when someone asked I should say that my surname was

Riglos but it was too late because the lady who asked me knew it was a lie but my work, I thought, would be appreciated even if my surname was López but I didn't say anything to the professor and the esteem I felt for him fell several rungs.

The exhibition lasted a week and I sold ten paintings but I noticed people were cold toward me I don't know if they were cold exactly but something told me I would never be a part of the group which was a relief because I needed time to study and paint. I wasn't good for anything else, not even untying knots or opening bottles.

Fortunately the newspapers covered the event and I didn't notice but a photographer took my photo which appeared in the newspaper next to my work *Disappointment*.

Disappointment is a long strip of a smoky color descending into a lake full of feathers and rose petals with a background in blurry reddish tones and to me represents a passage from *Hamlet*, when Ophelia drowns in the lake.

When I describe my work I speak like an artist but only inside otherwise I would taint the meaning I wanted to bring into the world.

Later I took part in other more important exhibitions under the pseudonym Riglos which is to say Yuna Riglos and the professor always accompanied me and once he promised that we'd go to Europe if things went well.

I still hope to go to Europe but alone because I have arrived at the conclusion that it's better to look after yourself although I will never forget what I owe to the professor because I'm not an ingrate which is the worst thing a person can be in addition to selfish and envious, I come across people like that wherever I go but it isn't my fault I'm so brilliant at the art of painting and I'm sure that I am because a gentleman described me as the Pettoruti of the day and I've been to exhibitions by that painter and was amazed.

The professor who is my representative said that if I continue to sell in two or three years I'd be able to buy a small apartment and that it wasn't good to grow up depending on your family or be like him who at the age of forty-something didn't have a home of his own.

I buy books with artistic images and I've fallen in love with Picasso and the French pointillists and have decided that when I can I shall go to Paris to visit the Louvre. For now, my nineteen years of age are keeping me in the house of a mother who will be retiring from teaching soon and sometimes sits on the patio watching night fall and I know that she's remembering Father who never came back. Maybe he's dead or who knows what . . .

My efforts allow me some control and fluency over my conversation. Not entirely but if I continue on like this and read books every night maybe I won't be different anymore although I doubt it and I don't care. There's a boy who looks at me and rides around on a bicycle he isn't well dressed you can tell he's

poor and works as a builder or well digger. I say that because of
the stains on his clothes and the roughness of his hands . . . but
he's very handsome and when he looks at me his eyes gleam,
they're the color of honey and he looks like Gary Cooper in the
film *High Noon* and I wait for him to pass by on his bicycle and
if I'm going to the School of Fine Art he tries to come over and
calls me small but beautiful and one night I painted more than
usual without getting tired because maybe I was in love but I'd
never say so and especially not to Petra who told me disgusting
things and would laugh at me or think that I practiced the sexual act . . . never no one will ever know about the skinny boy on
the bicycle because the things that happen between a man and a
woman are disgusting and I'd never survive it. Instead I'll walk
different streets to avoid the skinny boy on the bicycle because
I remember what my dead grandma, the mother of my mother,
said. She said that man is fire and woman straw the devil comes
and blows and because of how inflammable straw is that's it and
I know that I shall cry if I can tonight because I keep my word
and I shall never see the skinny boy on the bicycle again. But on
a canvas I shall paint the burning in his eyes, a beauty I'll never
see the likes of again . . . And so that's the way things are. The
tiredness you already know about obliges me to stop writing for
now but I'll be back.

When Petra Accomplishes Her Goal

I had been so busy recently that I barely spent any time at home, only to eat unless I had a light snack out. So I lost track of Petra, Betina, Aunt Ingrazia, Danielito, and Rufina because I was flitting around like a bird to fulfill my commitments. It's a pity I was never able to give talks because of my difficulties with the spoken word and the empty deserts that formed in my head where inspiration from objects and subjects feelings or allegory were formed that I then poured into my works because I was a nexus (from the dictionary) between something and someone, something creative that could not be denied, bursting forth like a spring.

One afternoon Petra came to tell me that what she had suggested to the neighbor was occurring, one night he jumped, the next she climbed and they always practiced you know what and my apologies but I am a frank writer.

I asked Petra if she felt love for the neighbor and she said that she felt love for the memory of Carina which is to say her sister who was impregnated by the potato oaf and he was sure that she adored him because to practice you-know-what one needs to be deeply in love otherwise he'd stop loving her and think she was a prostitute which means that the potato man had some notion of morality, but the fact that he took advantage of the angelical Carina cast everything to the dirty floor of the barn he shared sometimes with Petra.

And then six more months passed in addition to the year since the jumping and climbing exercise began and one day in the evening as usual Petra came and I saw she was looking pale but I won't say afraid because the Lilliputian dwarf wasn't afraid of anything and I think that if she'd committed a crime like for example poisoning the wife of the potato neighbor she'd have no trouble scuttling away into a crack like a cockroach. But still she did seem nervous and I saw that she kept her little monkey hand in her pocket and when she saw me looking she took it out and fiddled with her hair but I wasn't convinced by her exaggerated show of calm performed by moving her hand from one place to another looking to see if it was working which it wasn't and again I begged her not to hurt or even think of hurting the potato woman who was as innocent as Carina even if she was old and common and Petra swore on the memory of the dead girl and the baby that she'd never considered hurting the potato woman, she'd not even thought about it and that reassured me.

Only now do I know that I'm not very intuitive.

The Despair of the Neighbor's Wife,

Which Shocked the Neighborhood

That night I went to bed at midnight but hadn't yet got to sleep when I heard the cries of the neighbor which is to say the wife of the potato man whose turn it was that night to wait for Petra to do you-know-what and along with the woman's screams I heard a knock at my bedroom door and it was Petra who went straight to my little bathroom to wash herself and certain undergarments. I don't think anyone heard her frantic visit and I went into the bathroom and she was in the bath soaping herself and I saw that the water was pink like when you clean chicken legs and Petra said, Close the door, we're going spend the night together and tomorrow you have to say that I slept here all night, and I said I would but she needed to promise me that the blood didn't belong to the neighbor's wife and she swore it didn't.

As I'd heard the woman's screams I concluded that she was not the casualty (dictionary).

I helped Petra wash until we'd wiped away every trace of blood and her clothes too which we hung out to dry by the stove and when I picked up her coat a penknife fell out of the pocket which I put in the bath and Petra told me to put on rubber gloves and wash the penknife again although she said it was a Sevillian navaja and I believed her. I dried the folding blade and wrapped it in newspaper.

Later Petra called Aunt Ingrazia, her mother, and said we'd been out walking and as it was late she'd stay at my house and help me clean up my paint-spattered room and she begged me if anyone asked if she had stayed the night to say that she had and to repeat everything she'd told her mother because otherwise she'd be in trouble and we went to bed because we were both very tired.

But because I couldn't get to sleep I got up made two paintings on cardboard, one called *Nude Dwarf* and the other *Dressed Dwarf* and just in case anyone doubted that she'd been at my house the day and night before there was the proof that Petra didn't just help me but she also posed as a model for her painter cousin who was known and respected in the world of fine art. Now I suspected the horrors I'd read about the next morning in the newspaper but out of discretion I didn't ask and also out of pity for the memory of the late Carina and her baby.

And so Petra got up and drank her mate and was amazed
at her portraits, letting out little squeals like a monkey at the
zoo, and I told her that if she was interrogated she should say
that she'd posed almost all night and she hugged me and said
you're a genius and we continued to drink our mate with pas-
tries until midday when we opened the newspaper which I'd
already flipped through telling Petra she needed to read the
news without letting on any foreknowledge (dictionary) and we
shouldn't say anything about the bloody episode but because we
lived close by we went out to watch when a bag we assumed or
rather knew contained a body was sensationally brought out to
the ambulance.

The newspaper contained a horrifying article and a photo
of the neighbor lying on the floor of the barn with the potatoes,
yams, vegetables, flowers, and fruit in a huge pool of blood
with his legs spread and mouth stuffed with his penis and other
things that Petra whispered to me were testicles which the vul-
gar call balls or nuts but the anatomical term is testicles. The
neighbor had all that in his mouth and his groin was ragged
like a cloth you throw away because it's too worn to be of any
use. Next to it was a photo of his wife pulling her hair in despair
and you couldn't hear the screams because photographs don't
let you but you could guess from how the poor woman's mouth
was open just like the whole neighborhood heard that night and
Petra looked at me and said, How awful, that poor good man,

who could have committed such an atrocity, meaning who had messed him up like that, and I looked at her impassively and said who knows and we folded the newspaper for Mother, the professor, and Rufina to read.

I walked Petra back home to show Aunt Ingrazia which is to say Petra's mother the portraits and ask permission for Petra to stay with me for a few days because I wanted her to pose and inspire me because her difference made her interesting and thus very marketable to which Ingrazia agreed very happily because it's right for cousins to be friends and my company would be very good for Petra.

I had the navaja in my pocket wrapped in newspaper and Petra told me that she'd taken it from her father Uncle Danielito's toolbox and when they were otherwise distracted I went and slipped it back where it belonged without touching it.

The neighborhood was shocked and the vicious nature of the crime led people to believe that it must have been out of vengeance.

How awful we said but no more and we went to offer our condolences to the family of the tragically deceased potato, yam, vegetable, flower, and fruit man and the widow kissed us thank you and gave us a dozen satsumas.

Enough. The incident was never brought up again although the police went from house to house asking questions. But given the lack of suspects in the neighborhood and because the gentleman was Italian they labeled it a vendetta, which means revenge in Italian, and I quietly said to myself that that was exactly what it was and a couple of weeks later everyone had forgotten about the potato man.

And so Petra joined the other inhabitants of the house which between the professor, me, and my mother's pension we'd made quite different and Betina had a room to herself which allowed her to settle her soul tail which seemed to have stopped growing, leading me to the conclusion that she might not die so soon after all and she seemed happier with the candy and chocolates and gifts that the professor brought her because he'd grown fond of her but when he tried to teach her to write he failed because Betina shoved a pencil in his eye, just playing, not maliciously, and the good professor's eye went red.

Close by Mother's which is to say our house was and still is Saavedra Park where I now went quite regularly to paint, sitting on one of the marble benches from where I could admire the fountain with the cherubs (dictionary) and also could see a small bridge and a statue of an angel holding a fish and also other statues and one of Saavedra who I was taught was a founding father but I don't remember what he did. History was never easy for me, in fact none of the subjects were, except for drawing and painting.

One Saturday I went to sit on a bench with cardboard to paint the fountain not ordinary as it looked but how I felt

it inside and little wings had already sprouted against a lilac
background with blue lightning bolts and a very white plat-
form where I planned to paint little portraits of barefoot children spattered with gold from the stars and the faint glow of
the waxing moon the moon that looks like a plucked eyebrow
like you see on the faces of movie stars and elegant women and
in a year I'll pluck my eyebrows the same way even though the
professor told me that my eyebrows are well proportioned for
my features and if I plucked them I'd lose personality and my
personality was stunning so long as I didn't speak too much
because I had a strange way of expressing myself and it might
make listeners smile and they'd know even if they didn't say so
about my handicap and knowing my cousins among whom one
without a defect was rare they'd conclude that I wasn't normal
and even worse would lose interest in my paintings and at night
in the mirror with the tweezers in hand and feeling the touch
of the cold steel I didn't dare because the professor was always
right and I owed everything I'd achieved to him and I loved
him with respect like a father and if my father was with us I'd
also love him like that but he abandoned us and I could barely
remember him.

And while I pondered (idem) this nonsense I thought I saw
at the corner of the Children's Hospital a stroller pushed by a
gentleman who looked similar to the professor but the professor
looked like any other gentleman pushing a stroller he must have

come out of the hospital where as we know children are treated for health problems.

And so I sat still looking in that direction because if the gentleman had gone into the hospital I'd see him come out and I sat for quite a long time with the unfinished paintings and didn't see anyone come out of the medical building.

Remember that when I add periods I need to rest and the space in my head fills up with shapes and ideas that will never come out if I keep staring at the dot. I'll take a rest.

It was twilight now and not cold because we were a month into spring according to the calendar and the trees were dressing themselves up in leaves and flowers and I liked the orange blossom and acacia. The shrubs and some of the linden blossoms were coming to life and when I looked the other way I added some greens and yellows, but yellow brings me bad luck so I stopped the yellow, adding a faint pink like water when you wash blood from a wound, and I felt a cold shiver remembering Petra's pink water and our adventure that I swore to forget but I couldn't. I sometimes dreamed of the adventure and the satsumas that were given to us by the widow of the man who jumped where Petra climbed and I managed step by step to convert the object into something subjective which is to say created by me and now maybe because it was night I got a little scared and stood up from the bench to leave the park and walk home slowly.

And so I was walking down a street, stopping at the corner to check for vehicles, and I saw on the parallel (idem) street a gentleman pushing a stroller and that gentleman was my professor and the stroller he was pushing contained Betina who was eating honey popcorn and laughing hard in her deep voice because Betina was small but she had a man's voice which she used for the few words she'd learned, to ask to go piss and poo and for food, and now she was laughing and laughing while the professor whistled a barcarole that sounded like a lullaby and I saw the tail that Betina dragged behind her which poked out from the gap between the back of the stroller and the seat and it bounced along in time to the professorial whistle, which is to say she was dancing and in the middle of the tail which was in fact a soul that seemed to have stopped growing throbbed a blood red rose that, although it embarrasses me to write it I must because I am writing frankly, didn't just look like but was the blood from her now fully active privates and I had to sit down on the curb because I would never, never have imagined that the professor was capable of such behavior just like the man you know who and which I won't describe. But still I told myself that my imagination was playing tricks on me and it was just a painting in the spring twilight air with its dizzying perfume. I decided to continue on my way and not say anything to anyone because I was already used to that because of the experience you already know about and I shall never repeat again.

I need a rest. I got home and went to my room to finish the painting and added two more feet and two wheels in front of it and in the middle of the composition put a big red bleeding rose whose petals burned by an evil heat were falling into the lilac blue background.

Now Petra was also sleeping in my room because she had moved her bed there with the help of a boy from the neighborhood and we shared a wardrobe. She also brought a radio.

The house had changed in appearance because now it had everything it needed and we ate well although I preferred to eat out so I could think and avoid Betina's guzzling because she was getting hungrier and hungrier and also Mother's sad face as she was eating less and less and the professor who along with Rufina rushed around serving and cooking and taking a place that had been empty but that would have belonged to my father even though he'd abandoned us. As my cognitive abilities grew so did my capacity for curiosity and feeling and I always knew that I'd never know where my father was but if it weren't for him I wouldn't be painting and earning quite a lot of money and I could even buy a calfskin coat in a famous fur store in my city which looked lovely on me and I knew that it looked lovely on me because of the compliments I received from the gentlemen when I left the School of Fine Art and I'd got used to eating out and some people stared at me because they knew that I was the painter Yuna Riglos but you already know that Riglos was made up by the professor so that my cardboards and canvases would be worth more because that's what humans are like and if I signed Yuna López, I wouldn't sell so many and people would say, Oh, I bought a Riglos.

I need a rest.

It felt wonderful when people said I bought a Riglos as though they were saying I bought a Pettoruti or a Degas. Also the professor, and this was good for me, didn't tell me what color or composition I had to paint and he always encouraged me and found me places to exhibit and once I was on the cover of an arts magazine and I came out so pretty that the professor told me I looked identical to the Modigliani girl in the black tie I mentioned before and I was so happy that I almost jumped on top of him like I used to before when he started teaching me and then he said stop it because my breasts were growing—not much because I was always skinny—but my status had changed because I wasn't a girl I was a young lady and you know what I mean.

Rest.

Seeing as the professor was now living with us I should say his name I don't know why I didn't do it before I felt related to him and I will say his name which was José and his surname was Camaleón. José Camaleón, the professor, was now in charge quite a lot of the time in a house of women or half-women because each of us was missing something or had some other failing.

As for Petra the news was that she painted herself like a door and looked like a figurine on a birthday cake, fluttering here and there with long eyelashes and big lips and cheeks because she painted red circles on her cheeks as though she wasn't naturally rosy already enhancing the sensation that she'd slapped the makeup on with a roller.

When it came to her outfit, she said, she'd be sexier because I paid her fifty pesos a month to clean my room and wash my underwear, run errands and things and she had to go to a fine seamstress because clothes weren't made in her size and I watched her change and was happy to see her so happy and was certain that no man could deceive her because you know that she knew . . .

Part Three

The Barbecue's Debut

I can't get used to calling the professor Don José even though
he told me to and if I wanted to just call him José I could because he felt like part of the family even though he only knew
Aunt Ingrazia and Uncle Danielito in passing so Mother decided to hold a gathering in the backyard where Don José had
installed a fancy new barbecue and a long table and two long
benches and wicker chairs. We had everything one needed,
even a fire which we fed with wood from old railway sleepers
sold by the widow of the deceased man you know about and
so with other supplementary accessories (from the dictionary)
the barbecue would be finger-licking good and when he said
that I was struck by a wave of nausea (idem) that ran through
my whole body almost making me vomit, but I didn't. Recently

some words had been making me feel sick because of events from the past that unfortunately never completely leave you and ruin your day however splendid (idem) it might be.

I think the dictionary is good for me, I think that I will overcome difficulties that I previously found impossible and I don't let on what's on my mind which is that if I get over all my handicaps I will go to live on my own because all these people are tiring and my sight is as profound as my speech is superficial and I don't like what I see in the depths and it will hurt less at a distance or I won't care because every second I drift further away from what they call family and every second I think more about myself.

I bought a big canvas on which to paint my world.

Yellow brings me bad luck and I'm superstitious but here it's going to be indispensable (dictionary) like for certain painters who later suffered from bouts of madness and suicide, the former in my case is inevitable because my family leaves a lot to be desired but the latter depends on me so I won't let it happen.

For the premiere of the barbecue pit Don José chose Betina's birthday which is September 20, the last day of winter because the first day of spring is the 21st. Betina became someone from the moment the choice was made.

Betina was sitting in her little high chair in the sun playing with toothpicks on the enamel high chair tray, but I looked closer and saw they weren't ordinary toothpicks but rather small sticks you could use to make little houses, benches, and other everyday things but Betina's arms were so short that to put something to the left she had to tilt her whole body in that direction and the same to the right and her construction fell apart.

She kicked but her little legs were so short they hit fresh air and then she cried out upset—if not furious—and it made sense because she wanted to create something and she couldn't because she was completely handicapped although her soul tail had shrunk considerably and I thought she was looking quite a lot better.

I was something like a year older than her and when someone said so they'd say it couldn't be true but it was.

Betina didn't speak much but sometimes she could express herself through a whole phrase like the time she shouted out what was happening when her development came and because she was scolded afterward maybe she spoke less and preferred instead to harummm so she wouldn't be scolded but if she dared, and if what I had seen on the parallel street wasn't my imagination maybe Betina could have explained situations that I sensed but because flies can't get into open mouths I didn't say anything about it and although I noticed changes in the little monster which is what Betina was, in fact, I could have gone to my mother calm and collected to tell her what I thought I saw that evening and the ways in which Betina and someone else who I won't name for now were acting. But I'll talk all this over with Petra and we'll see what comes out of all this mess.

Petra was waxing the floor of our bedroom when I called her and she said she was coming and kept on waxing until she was done. She went off to wash her hands and came over to find out what was going on.

I told her that I'd noticed a change at home and in how the people who lived there which included the two of us were acting and she drying her hands on her apron said that it made sense, thanks to the money the house was fixed up and there was always very good food. It was a shame I was always eating out, if not I'd have noticed the effort José made especially with Betina who she thought was so round that her tray was pressing down on her belly and I told her about the soul tail in great detail and she said that was just an artist's nonsense and all artists were strange and half-crazy and that I shouldn't get angry but I too counted among that species and she'd have given ten centimeters of her stature just to be a painter or sculptor and although she wasn't complaining she knew that people called her a Lilliputian dwarf and she put up with it because everyone was how their whore mother made them and that was that. I need a rest.

I realized that she was a little offended even though I was the one who should be offended because of what she'd said about being strange and half-crazy but Petra didn't even reach my waist and she was pitiable enough already. She didn't deserve to be told off or hear coarse words.

Poor Petra, she did so much extra work to avenge Carina's shattered innocence she must carry so much sorrow inside her and I only recently noticed it, because she was born a dwarf and would be one until she died so I stroked her little head and asked where she was going this afternoon and she said to work. I asked her if she needed a raise of ten or twenty pesos if I sold the big painting which was almost finished but she refused because she earned a lot practicing her trade, she said.

What trade I asked and in a sardonic (dictionary) voice she said the oldest in the world although without oral sex because it made her nauseated and she didn't need any of her customers to experience absolute ecstasy because she wasn't planning on cutting off any of their penises. She hadn't been hurt by any of her customers because they wore condoms during their amorous sessions. She fetched her bag and took out some balloons made of latex or whatever and told me all kinds of things urging me never to make love without insisting that the gentleman in question use the balloons some of which were different colors and when she blew one up I realized where it was supposed to go on the gentleman customer as Petra called them. And the image of the skinny boy on the bicycle appeared in the mist of my inspiration and I got the giggles because I imagined him putting one where he was supposed to put it and the feeling of longing that sometimes took me by surprise faded away like sand slipping through your fingers and the skinny boy who looked like the Gary Cooper of my teenage yearnings (idem) was also nothing in the nothing of my hand with the sand and he flew away forever and I was glad of that because as much as it embarrasses me, what had been a romantic wound after the moment with the latex became just a ridiculous source of disgust from which I was safe thanks to my inherited handicap, which had actually turned out to be useful.

I asked Petra what time she would be back and she said that she had to meet four customers but they were all old married fools and she had to help one of them pull up his pants when he was done so she'd be back in two or three hours because before she'd pass by the market to buy a leg of lamb to roast out back along with potatoes and yams that she'd buy from the widow you already know about.

She went out with a red dress, white shoes, and a white purse with red trim and she'd permed her hair making it look like a swimming cap, covered in makeup like I've already described—forgive my criticism—she looked like one of the monkeys they sell at the entrance to the zoo which are made of plaster and dog hair, which have become traditional in our city and almost every child asks their parents to buy them along with peanuts to give to the flesh-and-blood monkeys in the cages. I don't go to the zoo much because animals were born to be free all of them especially birds. My heart can't stand their pleading (idem) gazes which say save me from these horrible days and nights and I can't do anything for them, they're victims of human ignorance. I need a rest.

If I weren't half-handicapped I wouldn't need to rest but as I've already said each indispensable (idem) period and comma fills my head with incredible visions and thoughts that overwhelm me and hurt my brain I think it's my brain that hurts and my brain is the sickest and weakest of my entire useless family's and I shouldn't say things like that but sometimes I wish I were completely normal.

But each of us is how they were born and you just have to put up with it the way I put up with the fake surname of Riglos which the professor, known as Don José Camaleón or just José, put underneath my paintings. I can't get used to seeing him in his shirtsleeves reading the newspaper or drinking mate as if he owned the house and although it seems rude I say to myself that that role belongs to my father who lost it because he abandoned us but I have no right to ask things that are none of my business and also I was the one who first brought the professor home when we were poor and the house didn't have a backyard with a barbecue pit and Petra wouldn't be able to roast meat and delicious chinchulines when she got back from the oldest profession, and other times too.

I finished painting the canvas, in oil paint this time, and it came out so beautifully that it was a shame to sell it but I was proud to make a living from my work, it paid for my upkeep at a home that day by day and I don't know why seemed more and more remote more theirs than mine because I was a languid (idem) shadow that sometimes floated around indoors and the environs (idem). Let me explain idem means dictionary but it's easier because it's shorter and because I never take what's not mine I have to say that the word arises out of my cultural research with the dictionary which is helping me to overcome my inherited handicap.

Betina's Birthday Party

José had got the fire going in the barbecue and the backyard
was full of family members coming and going who were
joined by Aunt Ingrazia and Uncle Danielito who saw Petra
their daughter when she arrived laden with packages and bags,
dropping the meats you already know about on the table before
taking bottles of white and red wine from a box and some nonalcoholic drinks and bread and everything giving rise to a rapid
calculation that she must have worked very hard because the
things she'd brought weren't cheap, they were exquisite—the
fruit for sangria looked like paintings of still lifes, especially
the grapes and the apples. After trimming excess parts from
the leg of lamb, José put it on the grill surrounded by blood
sausage, chorizos, tripe, and chinchulines, he knew how to

cook an asado and while he was toiling away he drank wine to
get in the mood and the other guests started to lay a big table
with the boards on which one traditionally savors (dictionary)
these meats and the forks and knives and matching trays, all
of Mother's crockery came out to gleam in the light from the
string of bulbs, all of which were lit and a few thick candles as
decoration and there were also different colored balloons floating around and I thought it looked like a Christmas party but
no it was just Betina's birthday, she was asleep in her cot even
though she was going to turn eighteen all told that night, but
in my house everything was different because it was us each
with our own limitations, character, and status. Music was playing from Petra's radio and just then Ortiz Tirado was singing,
Kiss me . . . kiss me plenty . . . as though tonight were our
last . . . and I can't remember how it went on but I went on because my brain is tired, I think it must be like the brains on the
barbecue sizzling away, my poor brain of which I ask too much
and now I feel more like going to bed than joining the party and
said so to Petra who got angry because she said I had no right
to escape just because I was a bit tired when she was genuinely
exhausted after practicing the oldest profession and instead of
four customers she'd serviced five and to cap it all off the last
had been quite young and left her lying on the bed and she'd felt
like staying on her work bed but decided she had to do her duty
and went to the market.

I need to rest.

I had to take a good long rest because in addition to Petra's revelations there was my hurry to finish the painting and shower and get myself ready and I asked Petra if she was going to shower and get ready because she'd come back looking quite messy and she said she'd do it but just for her because she was feeling sorry for herself and I felt sad and gave her a kiss on her funny little face with its running, slobbered-over colors. Petra hugged me hard and sighed, Why were we even born . . . and I answered that we were born because a couple got the urge and didn't use condoms and she said that she'd always use them so as not to bring degenerate children into this bitter degenerate world and still hugging we cried an ocean of tears like we never had before me crouching down because otherwise we'd never have managed the special embrace and sobbing which intensified and wetted the gathering dusk and did us both good.

The radio sang with Ortiz Tirado's romantic voice another melody about the last night I spent with you and I washed my face telling myself to stop crying while Petra got undressed and into the bath and I saw bruises darkening the skin of her sorry little body and one or two bite marks and scratches or something similar and I didn't say anything but I did almost burst into tears but I contained myself.

The bruises and other wounds on the little woman inspired some painful compositions that I wouldn't be able to paint that night but would the next day, and for some reason I called them *Las Magdalenas* although there weren't any women in them but I'd decided that both the cardboard and the canvas would sob the way we had in our embrace and that people would see the works and shiver without knowing why.

I went out to the backyard and in the light from the fire in the barbecue the professor or José whichever you prefer to call him was wielding the pointy two-pronged piece of iron to rearrange the hunks of meat which shocked me a little and he was sweating because it was hot and the sweat ran down his naked torso because he'd taken off his shirt and I saw the hair on his chest and under his arms too and I said to myself I hope I don't vomit because it would ruin Betina's party, she was now sitting at the head of the table and beating her enamel tray with a fork and knife and although I tried to ignore it I heard her little farts and looked at Petra and we decided to sit at the other end of the table in case of unwanted accidents or in case we started giggling or laughing or who knew what she might come up with during the course (idem) of the gathering and we didn't want to be the harpies of the party.

José said that he'd invited another teacher, of mathematics, who was a lonely widower and although he had a son and daughter they didn't live with him. I knew the teacher of mathematics by sight although I'd never spoken to him and he had a smile as big as the girth (idem) of a watermelon and was always

smiling and at the School of Fine Art he taught drawing and
never failed any of his students. He might come with his girlfriend, said José, who was a beautiful girl with green eyes and
a very elegant dresser although the professor wasn't but we'd
like him because he was so friendly and well-mannered and
I thought it was a little off key to introduce strangers to the
group, José was already enough and I don't know why I now
saw him as an outsider when I hadn't before and Mother and my
aunt and uncle were all here and no one else was missing when
José's guests arrived Petra whispered in my ear that the professor was rude to introduce his acquaintances to the family. But
that was what happened and we would allow it as far as the rim
of the glass but not if it overflowed (idem).

The boards started to circulate and get filled up and the
glasses got filled too and I looked at Betina who although she
was waving around her fork and knife needed help to eat because she had to have her food cut up for her and brought to her
mouth which was packed with ogre teeth.

José Camaleón the Professor's Guests

When José's guests arrived at the party every face turned to the entrance and saw the mismatched couple that were the guests, they didn't have enough eyes in their faces to take in all the members of our huge family although both had two eyes that together made four green eyes, the woman's very pretty the man's ugly and beady and he was shorter than her too, the common ratty type one often sees on the street or sitting or standing in administrative offices but this was the drawing teacher I already mentioned at the school and he also played other roles I can't remember now, and she worked as a model for clothes and cosmetics and was very well dressed although my capacity for introspection (dictionary) told me something that wasn't obvious at first sight and something similar was true of the gentleman who wasn't elegantly dressed, and I got goose bumps and felt an urge to leave where I was sitting next to Petra who was elbowing me to make sure that I didn't miss a detail—she was sitting on three cushions piled on the wicker seat so she could reach the table.

Let me rest.

And suddenly I realized that on the other side of my chair, the other side from Petra there was an empty seat and the pretty woman was sitting next to José and so the gentleman guest who'd come with the girl with the green eyes came to sit next to me in the empty seat and with a big smile asked permission to sit down and said how he'd got lucky, and I didn't understand but Petra asked what luck that might be and he answered to be sitting next to such a pretty girl who of course would be me. Was me. Naturally I didn't say anything and Petra answered for me that he was indeed lucky, My cousin is an artist by the name of Riglos, and the gentleman said, Riglos the painter, my goodness how marvelous, and he tried to kiss me on the cheek but I shook my head the way wet dogs do and the gentleman pretended not to notice and went on smiling under his big bristly mustache which covered his mouth but not his breath which smelled of earlier meals whose remnants (idem) still lurked in the gaps between his teeth. I didn't know whether I could take it and I said to Petra, Come, sit next to the gentleman seeing as you're in a talkative mood, and Petra said she could talk and see fine from where she was but I insisted and she got worried that I'd vomit, it was about to come up, and swapped places and as she was a woman of the world she had the gentleman put the cushions onto my seat which would now be hers which the gentleman did reluctantly something I could tell because his mustache drooped down.

Let me rest.

The gentleman tried to look past Petra to talk to me about pictorial art and drawing and Petra suggested that he relax and try to enjoy the shindig, it's my opinion that Petra's common vocabulary is a result of the kind of job she did and I think that it grated on the gentleman because little by little he spoke less so I intervened (idem) and asked him if the pretty young woman was his girlfriend and he said, We're on that path but . . . nothing serious because she's divorced and has daughters and I'm widowed and have children and it's complicated. I suggested he look across the table to see how happy the chic (idem) divorcée seemed talking to José Camaleón and the man didn't like that and Petra added that between him and José the lady suited José better while he was a better match for her because he was so short albeit not Lilliputian and if the lady agreed they could announce both matches then and there but the gentleman said no.

I called over to José from my seat asking what the name of the woman he'd invited was and José reluctantly turned from the divorced woman and girlfriend of the gentleman sitting next to me at the table and said, Oh how rude . . . I didn't introduce

you . . . the young lady is called Anita del Porte and my friend
Abalorio de los Santos Apóstoles.

Everyone had to stifle a laugh over Abalorio de los Santos
Apóstoles but nobody let out a peep and they all continued gorg-
ing on their food and downing their wine and on my board several delicacies sat still waiting to be nibbled but my stomach had
turned over and my head was spinning with ideas for canvases
because now I used the cardboard for practice sketches and my
major exhibitions required expressive compositions resting or
dancing or suffering on fine large canvases that I would subsequently take to have framed in quality wood or metal depending on what the buyer or whoever wanted. Either Petra kept the
money for me or I deposited it in the bank. Petra advised me
never to tell anyone how much I had because it was a crooked
world, no place for the unwary, and I trusted Petra more than I
did myself because she contributed to the household much more
than she consumed, too much, to keep everyone's mouths shut
the same way sometimes people smiled and greeted me with
one of those kisses on the cheek in passing.

It so happened that Abalorio asked me how much the
painting entitled *Serenade to Autumn* was worth and I told him
one thousand five hundred pesos and he said that was what he
earned in six months in pedagogy and I asked about pedagogy
and he said secondary school math classes and when it came
to his private painting classes it would take him a year to earn

that much and Petra popped up like a grasshopper and whispered, My little cousin Yuna certainly has her charms but you, my dear, are better off sticking with the divorcée or with me, I don't earn half of what Yuna does but more than you, I think, seeing as you make such a show of being poor even though you're a professor and I practice the oldest profession in the world so I really shouldn't earn more than you and I'm looking for a worthy candidate for Yuna with cars and trips to Europe not because she couldn't obtain the luxuries mentioned without my help but because my cousin is a generous angel she could be taken in by anyone but I'm a prostitute so knowledgeable about dishonest matters and your nails are dirty from scratching yourself or scratching your girlfriend maybe she's all show and underneath has a spotty ass. And then she went quiet and I swear that Petra knew how to be discreet and her speech was for Abalorio's big ears only and he continued to smile but went white as a sheet and looked down at his dirty nails.

José got up from his chair to serve another helping of victuals (idem) on the boards and he didn't need to refill the glasses but did have to get more bottles because no one had left a drop and José asked me if I was all right and I looked at him with my face—just like the Modigliani girl with the tie—and that was enough because he didn't ask again.

The Toast

A case of champagne was brought in and I thought it rather common that they put it down right in the middle of the table next to the cake because all those bottles were a clear statement that no one here was shy of a drink and they knocked accidentally against the three-layer cake and it collapsed into a single layer with two more on the tablecloth and I realized that at three layers the cake was bigger than Betina the birthday girl and that the case of liquor knew what it was doing and a portrait of Betina meant a beheaded cake and a doll with its arms and legs broken off and I asked permission to go to my room to jot down an impression (idem) of my experiences on cardboard and I knew the painting I'd make when I had time would win a national or international award. I was confident and in the end got back quickly from the sketch to the party where they were toasting Betina's eighteen years although she never got to cut the cake which was served in lumps on plates and no one complained except for Betina who greedily cried more . . . more . . . more!!! She ate desserts with her hands and occasionally managed to get them into her fat mouth crying, Yummy!!! Yummy!!! Yummy!!! but something was bothering the girl that night, she was staring at José with an expression that looked both angry and hurt and I imagined that it must be concatenated (idem) to José's very friendly attitude to the divorcée Anita del Porte but decided that it must be my imagination and I hoped it was because it was obvious that Abalorio de los Santos was in love with the lady with green eyes and if she swapped him for another he'd collapse in several ways and directions and Petra winked at me while she took Abalorio de los Santos's hand and in a bright, playful voice said I've just asked for Abalorio de los Santos's hand in marriage because we make a fine couple and I earn more than he does and that way we can reunite the estranged family he's been telling me about, bringing his children back into the family fold, not this overpopulated house but his apartment and we'll be happy forever after and Abalorio de los Santos will be able to drink wine whenever he wants and sing songs in the street and I promise to wash his clothes and clean his nails and trim his mustache and do tricks to make sure that the sex isn't the

nonsense boring church-married couples do and I saw poor
Abalorio de los Santos take from his breast a little chain with
a medal of the Virgin on it and kiss it and I saw him say to the
girlfriend with the green eyes, Let's go, and they left.

Let's toast Betina's wonderful eighteen years, Petra cried
and everyone toasted and Betina was happy because the divorced
girlfriend had left and José had gone back to doting on her.

I went to look outside and saw Anita del Porte and Abalorio
de los Santos Apóstoles get into a rather outdated car that Anita
drove while Abalorio lay in the back to sleep off the wine and I
said to myself what a pair of fools, such clowns, or maybe it was
just me. My imagination plays tricks but it's Petra who shines
a light on things for me and we'd subsequently talk it over because I still felt sorry for little Abalorio.

I don't know if I mentioned before that Mother and my
aunts had two brothers both bachelors and if I didn't say so I
add it here because I don't like to be unfair and family means
everyone or no one even though I'm going to move as soon as I
can and go overseas as soon as I can, and now I shall say something about the two uncles who were almost forgotten because
of the little they do to attract attention to themselves because
they're bachelors and pensioners and take long siestas, one of
them in his cot in a slum and the other under a bridge but they
both collect their pensions and don't have to beg, they live like
the birds of the field my communion priest told me about.

Uncle Pedrito and Uncle Isidorito were twins and they weren't very bright but they earned a living for themselves as public employees and the one who had the most difficulties was Isidorito because Aunt Ingrazia told me that all he was good for was moving files from one archive or office to another and after shuffling around like that for years he received the minimum pension but Isidorito had few wants and never got married so with his lack of commitments he lived well and Uncle Pedrito was a civil servant of the kind that holds hearings (idem) for people who need to see the authorities to file petitions without prior censure (idem) and he gave out envelopes containing permits until he retired and went to live in a very poor neighborhood and he was a bachelor too and called himself single and in no hurry but I wondered who would be in a hurry to get married to Uncle Pedrito who was ugly and crooked as a nightmare.

And because we hadn't seen them for quite a while, when they arrived they said they were very well and they met José Camaleón who was the big news, they kissed Betina and she slobbered over them because Betina kissed without swallowing her saliva but the recipients pretended not to notice and didn't take out their handkerchiefs to clean off the mucus and Betina be . . . be . . . be . . . happily clapped her hands because she liked being kissed it meant she was loved but I think they did it out of obligation. Definitely. And the ingrates who never

came to visit were questioned which was how we found out that
Isidorito preferred to live underneath the City Bell bridge close
to the city and that when it rained hard he went to Pedrito's
shack and they made fried buns and had barbecues and had got
into the bad habit of roasting chestnuts over a can and when the
cold worsened (idem) they lit a fire with a car tire very carefully so as not to burn themselves and the professor who now
regarded himself as lord and master of the house asked them
rudely whether they ever received visits from hookers meaning street women which didn't embarrass me because of Petra
although Petra would never visit such poor ugly customers as
Pedrito and Isidorito who at you-know-who's question went
red as a pair of tomatoes and after giving everyone their best
again left angry I think because they didn't come back and I
didn't go to visit them because I didn't know where the slum or
the bridge were but I painted a lovely painting I called *Estrange-
ment*, a word I chose carefully from the dictionary and came to
the conclusion that Don José Camaleón could separate us and
although I'd already decided to go that's not the same thing
as deciding that one must go because they have been slighted
(idem) and embarrassed.

Several hours later barely anyone was left by the barbecue
pit and the bottles were empty and some were asleep with their
heads on the table and others with their heads tipped back snoring and I who hadn't had a bite or drunk a drop of alcohol was

a faithful witness to events and I saw Petra go over to Betina
the birthday girl and frown then she came over to me and she
didn't say anything out loud at first then said something quietly
that I pretended not to hear with a gesture not entirely decent
but not indecent either and looked at Betina who was snoring
like a man and doing everything else into the contraption they
added below the chair which one could tell from the smell and
the splatter but it wasn't the poor thing's fault and it occurred to
me that few of us there had any reason to celebrate birthdays,
we should celebrate deaths given that by fulfilling our obligation to remain alive we were taking up space that might have
been occupied by a normal baby.

And when it was almost dawn, two more cousins arrived
I can't remember what the exact relationship was and left gifts
on behalf of I don't know who all wrapped up and on being
presented with the scene of sleeping guests they left and I don't
think they were real, they were a pair of ghosts of two cousins
whom I vaguely remembered but my memory is nonexistent, it
lives in the constant present because my imagination takes up
all of my brain and moves my arms and hands to paint.

I opened one package and found it was a bottle of champagne and opened the other and it was the same thing and then
Petra said let's take the bottles and not mention them to anyone to celebrate something in the future, we'll be sure to want
to some time. And fine, but it wasn't right. Whoever you are,

taking something that doesn't belong to you is stealing but what did it matter compared to the things Petra did for me and everything she taught me about the dangers of sexual activities and more.

I spent the rest of the night painting. Petra slept and cried in her sleep. Outside someone cleaned up, probably Rufina who said she preferred to do her chores (idem) right away and then sleep without interruption later. I did see Mother get up wearily and José pick up Betina and take her inside. And that was it.

Betina Needs a New Chair

When Betina was lifted out of her cot it was discovered that she had grown too fat for her chair.

She'd got so fat that it was easier to carry around both her and the chair together so a change was necessary if the poor girl was going to be comfortable and I decided to give her a new chair, not a high chair because the one I chose was large and pretty and I painted it with motifs that weren't childish at all because Betina was a young lady and the motifs were commented on by the family and were images of cheerfully colored flowers, butterflies, and nightingales and walking along an orange carpet came a little boy like baby Jesus with chubby little arms stretched out to be picked up and taken to the zoological gardens and the forest and nearby the baby I painted shadows

which I couldn't help because I have so many shadows inside
me that when I get overwrought (idem) I drive them out onto
my paintings but the shadows on Betina's chair didn't obscure
the baby because to me every baby is Carina's baby who came
to get her and took her away wrapped in a cloak of fever. No.
I would never burn a mother, not even in my imagination, or
torment a baby. I considered erasing the shadows. Then I left
them because landscapes always get darker and if my imagination continued in that vein (idem) it would get worse. I never
interfered with the dictates of my talent and imagination and
the talent part was written by an art critic in an article about me
and my work and that made me proud although I'm not vain the
way I thought that the woman with green eyes was vain and
before now a very long time ago Aunt Nené was when she made
fun of my adolescent cardboard paintings and thought she was
an artist making these big faces of ugly women with cows' eyes.
I realize that I'm learning to criticize with scorn (idem) and will
try to correct that tendency because it makes your soul ugly and
gives you wrinkles on your forehead and I don't want to have
wrinkles on my Modigliano model's face which I know is pretty
from the compliments people say in the street which didn't permeate before but now do and I should clarify that I should have
put *idem* after *permeate* because as you know I get the difficult
terms from the dictionary and until I am able to use them with
absolute fidelity I won't feel that they're fully my property and

forgive me if I'm boring you with all these explanations but I was born like this and I want to earn what I have honestly and not steal from anyone.

When I gave the decorated chair to Betina the poor thing who was always afraid of me because of what used to happen at mealtimes quite a long time ago shoving the spoon in her eye, ear, and everything before it got to her mouth and pushing her face into her soup and wishing her dead, she trembled and whimpered until she realized that I came with good intentions and stretched out her little arms to be put into her new chair and I should explain that I didn't forget that the chair required a recipient underneath for you-know-what to cater to her severe handicap. I put her in her new chair and she pointed to the pictures with her little fingers lingering over the image of the baby and said, Pretty baby, yes . . .

I immediately saw her fall into an intense reverie (idem) because Betina had a lot of conflicting emotions, for example that I had always ignored her and teased her in her childhood but now I was fussing over her pathetic person and had given her a gift which allowed her to stretch out as much as she wanted and breathe and her big belly seemed grateful to have the space it needed. I guessed, I don't know what I guessed because I might be very talented but I share being handicapped with Betina albeit to a minimal degree (idem). But I have to say that from the brand-new chair spread two smiles from two different mouths and I looked behind to see if the soul tail was there and it wasn't. It wasn't there and I said to myself that Betina had got her soul back, it wasn't slipping away anymore and maybe one of her problems would heal and she'd be less handicapped, at my level or something.

Once Betina had settled into her throne she started to finger it, discovering images and decorative motifs in her new surroundings, and I felt the feeling that comes with performing an act of charity for something or someone who isn't entirely human by which I mean different. Very different so much that it could scare someone taken unawares and to cap it all off Betina understood, she understood more than people taken unawares thought.

And now that she felt an iota (idem) of warmth from the hearth of her much-feared sister, me, she spoke to her new chair and suddenly she said, Yuna, why don't you give me a bed because I'll need one soon, and I felt inside my chest battered and bruised by ancient and continuous bouts of bronchitis, a bitter ocean crashing monstrous waves as monstrous as the two of us and I couldn't hold it back or tame it anymore, although later I'd paint it and I already had the title *Hidden Storms* and would exhibit it in gratitude or thanks to Betina who had kept hidden a full vocabulary and just then had taken the lid off a mysterious secret, she'd broken the hermetic seal of a horrendous terror, and I asked her to go on asking me for things because I had money and could set up a lovely bedroom with nightstands and mirrors and anything else she wanted and she grabbed my hand and shouted, Oh, a wicker crib.

I sat down on the floor and from there I could see how round Betina's belly was and went over and touched my sister's belly and she pressed my hand down over her belly with effort because her little arm was very weak but she did it and for the first and only time in my life I felt life and it was beautiful as the fluttering of a nightingale's wings when they drink nectar from a flower and Betina didn't let go so I could feel the rhythm of the breathing of something inside her with my sense of touch, my beautiful artist's hands, and Betina looked at me to see if I approved and I told her that I'd get the most elegant crib I could find and a silk-lined stroller and that we'd go out walking through the woods when the wolf wasn't there.

Exhausted, my ever so deformed and polite sister fell asleep and I sat petrified on the wooden floor looking at the belly and her appearance and adding what I saw to Petra's explanations and remembering that one should always wear condoms and what soulless men spurt into the woman's menstrual canal, how mysterious and chemically impossible for someone like me to take in the joining of tiny little floating living things that danced in incredible maternal waters and concatenated day by day slotting into one another like a magnificent puzzle until they had formed a creature, and just the thought of what Betina must be putting together made me shiver because we didn't bring anything good to the surface and even I, in spite of being the painter Riglos, hadn't been pardoned the category of strange and horrible being not on the outside but on the inside and I remembered Carina and swore that I wouldn't let anyone touch the baby because that was what Betina had in her belly, I wouldn't let them do what they did to Carina's baby who came back to take her away in the flames of a fever and they both were forgotten which is the only true death but I never forgot them.

It was midday and time to clean Betina and I'd fallen asleep on the floor but would take a shower and the others would do what they were accustomed (dictionary) to doing every day and life and lives would follow their courses because that's how it happens as much as those with ill intentions try to undermine (idem) essential truths.

When Rufina started her chores and the smell of food wafted from the kitchen I ran to the bathroom to take a shower and dress myself and I looked for my tools and rolled up canvases and left the hovel because I'd eat something out, close to the School of Fine Art and then I'd paint for as long as my strength held out in the studio I and other artists had rented.

I painted a great deal in a whirlwind. It rained and I saw thick drops on the panes and sat looking and came to the conclusion that big drops like the ones that fertilize nature are identical to the ones that rain just as eagerly into bellies for births similar to the budding of trees and gardens and that it wasn't right to call that trembling that song that magic sinful.

I stayed all night in the studio painting a little and sleeping a little until a crimson solar radiance hit me in the face.

Back at home—I call it that but I didn't feel it was my home anymore—we had a telephone which I used to call Petra. I arranged to meet her at the café in the Pasaje Dardo Rocha.

Conversation with Petra

While We Had Breakfast

I crossed the Diagonal 80 drunk on the city smells of petrichor and orange blossom but my sorrow on waking, I think I had dreamed bitter things, drove the fragrance away and I felt a cold spatter of newly fallen rain and shivered. When I went into the café Petra was there already sitting at the bar on a tall stool and I sat next to her and told her that I was very sad and worried. Petra had already ordered us a breakfast of white coffee and savory medialuna croissants. With her mouth full she asked, What's wrong with you, out with it or I'll get a stomachache, and Petra really did suffer from sharp pains in her stomach followed by vomiting because the poor thing had reason enough to float in a lake of disgust and nausea and I hurriedly told her that something very serious was happening to Betina and I was surprised that she who was always the first to know about things hadn't noticed and she said that she'd seen that she was fatter and uncomfortable in her little chair but she didn't even want to think what I was going to tell her because at night the ghost of the potato man came to her castrated and with his prurient (idem) parts dangling from the bestial slugs that stood in for lips in his swine mouth and Petra pushed aside her medialunas and assumed the same position as Rodin's *Thinker* although her interpretation was in miniature.

And she confessed to me that she avoided going near Betina and no one paid Betina any attention because she was the sorriest and most horrifying incarnation of our distorted (idem) and degenerate genes, caused by the evil eye or an inherited disease that one of her customers told her about called syphilis, and the descendants of the syphilitic were born dead or half alive like all of us, but if you wore a condom there was no danger of contagion and even if the children were born healthy they always needed to be checked because at any moment a virulent drop of what they called the French pox in Europe and after there was a war the soldier's pox might appear and although I'd never heard of this filth before I still decided to paint it allegorically and I told Petra off for telling people about our misfortune and she answered that it was nothing to be ashamed of, we weren't to blame for how our ancestors behaved and then she explained what ancestors meant.

Getting back to our talk about Betina, I noticed that my cousin was trembling and she remonstrated, Betina is your sister, Carina was my sister but I still asked her for advice because she was more worldly and Petra asked in a whisper if I thought that the same thing had happened to Betina as Carina and I told her that I did and asked her to please help. Petra almost screamed, I'm not doing it again—not for all the gold in the world—but I told her that doing the same thing would give her away and she'd end up in prison and what she'd done was completely forgotten although there was no such thing as a perfect crime and Petra said that doing justice isn't a crime.

I never thought of committing a crime and we both ordered another coffee and wondered who the degenerate who had interfered with Betina might be because if he was single we'd report him to force him to get married but what if he was married?

We'd decide about that later but Betina had asked for the crib with joy, maybe because small and horrendous as she was she had no notion of sin and we thought maybe Betina wouldn't even remember who it was but she never left the house so who could have made her belly if not a man of the house? Because we almost never held parties, Danielito was a married uncle to his cousin Ingrazia, both of them also my mother's cousins, and when we had the birthday party her belly was already round not as much as now but enough and we decided that that afternoon we'd take Betina out for a walk to debut her new chair and I'd make sure that by the time she got back she'd have the surprise of her new bedroom suite and crib waiting for her.

Suspicion

Suddenly we saw the professor come into the bar with the woman with the green eyes, Anita who had come to Betina's birthday party with her partner the shortie Abalorio de los Santos Apóstoles, which didn't seem unusual because Professor José Camaleón gave classes in the area and she did runway shows and had a makeup store nearby, but the unusual thing was the jolt it gave the professor when he saw us and we came to the conclusion that the only man we hadn't suspected was Professor José Camaleón and I felt my heart beat fast and began to sweat when I remembered the many times I'd seen him take Betina to her room and Petra said that we shouldn't be hasty because if what we suspected was true he'd move in with Anita del Porte the cosmetologist and whatever else, so we sat fiddling with our napkins and eventually waved hello in a friendly way and went on apparently making small talk but what we were actually talking about was slitting the throat of the accursed man, meaning that I had brought a curse on my house tragedy of tragedies.

When we got home we didn't say anything about what we'd seen at the café and went to Betina's bedroom calling Rufina to come and bathe her and make her pretty and when Betina heard "pretty" she smiled and was almost actually pretty and at one moment I asked Rufina if Betina was menstruating and she said she didn't know that people like Betina really menstruated and no but I knew that she had started before me and if it wasn't coming anymore then she was definitely pregnant and I asked Rufina how many months it had been since she had to wash my sister and she thought about it and answered six or seven, seven probably, and I felt like smacking Rufina who looked down on us from so high that she didn't even think of us as women capable of having babies in our bellies.

Betina's first walk in her decorated chair was a great joy for her while Petra and I were overcome with sadness.

Petra thought it necessary to hold a special family meeting to inform Mother of Betina's dangerous situation because a pregnancy of seven months in such a small body can't be fixed and I was relieved that Aunt Nené wasn't there to suggest something awful to preserve the family honor which would

have been too much for all of us and lunchtime came around
and I decided to stay because I'd be needed and I knew that
when something upset me I spoke more fluidly and came to the
conclusion that soon I wouldn't need the dictionary fount of so
much knowledge which taught me increasing my intuitive abilities and sometimes very clear concepts sprung forth with no
need to add idem meaning that they came from the dictionary
and that after flipping through the pages of the dictionary looking for the meaning of a term other words became clear and I
knew that one day I'd be the same as everyone else in the art
of speech.

José the professor arrived and inside I pictured him next to
Anita, he looked at me worried I'd say something about you-
know-what but I didn't.

It was October but the professor brought with him a pan
dulce and Christmas candy and I'm not putting idem because
I'm learning plenty and he had a rotisserie chicken that spread
its aroma around the room and said that he'd put it in the oven
to warm up and Petra said to set the oven on low otherwise
it would burn. Petra followed the professor into the kitchen to
peel the potatoes and yams, she knew how to caramelize the
yams I liked them more than the chicken and everything that
Petra did was good and wholesome except—and forgive me—
the oldest profession in the world which she did on the street, or
wherever she saw her six or seven customers. I'm trying for the

commas and periods not to make noises in my head and brain and I think that with effort I'm managing it and if the exercises I'm doing reading a text specializing in cases like the kind we suffer as a family, greater or lesser handicaps, I will resolve these annoyances which must hinder the reading of what I write and I offer a thousand apologies to you, reader, and if you are a believer you'll forgive me because the priest says forgive so that god will forgive you and I still have trouble with capital letters because of the scarring from the periods and I'm not familiar with a lot of other notions but I say again anything is possible with effort and you'll see that I'm right because I don't know what will happen during the meeting or how it will end and deep down I'm scared.

Mother was sitting under the grapevines staring into space, she looked like a chipped plaster statue. She had been a good teacher and used her pointer to straighten out more than a few and her retirement had crushed her, it had turned her into a soulless thing but when she walked around I looked to see if her soul was slipping out of her like it had with Betina, but no, so Mother was just sad and didn't feel like moving. She spent her days sitting under the grapevines and if someone spoke to her she smiled like a baby laughing because she didn't bother putting in her false teeth which were in a glass and disgusted me but I never told her that. This time I went over to Mother and asked her if she wanted lunch in half an hour or so, and she said that she did and I took the opportunity to ask whether she'd seen the bedroom I'd bought for Betina, and she asked why I'd gone to the expense, and my words burned more when I asked how she thought Betina was and she took a handkerchief out of her robe pocket and started to weep. I asked mother why she was crying, and with red eyes she said I knew why and I lied saying I didn't and if she wanted I could bring her her teeth to eat with, I could disinfect them and bring them to her, but she said no.

There were plenty of us at the table: in addition to my mother there was the professor, Petra, Betina, and me, as you can see I'm using more commas and my head doesn't buzz so much.

I forgot about Rufina who'd eat with us sitting next to me at my request and I had my reasons.

Rufina laid the oilcloth and big plates, glasses, and cutlery that mother saved for when someone got married or christened and any other important family event and Rufina set the table prettily because Petra had asked her to, and I agreed and told her that anything Petra told her to do she should because Mother wasn't good—forgive me for saying this—for anything anymore. All she was good for was sitting there with her chipped plaster face.

Rufina put a vase in the middle of the table with a bunch of lilies she'd bought with her own money which surprised us so much that we all gasped "Oh . . ." and then the professor arrived with the soup bowl because at home when we ate as a family, so to speak, Father served us from the soup bowl and since he'd left us we'd lost the habit it was like a legend that only at that moment reappeared out of such dark shadows that it seemed like a dream suddenly remembered but it would only have been a dream remembered if it was our father holding the ladle. When it was my turn I flipped over my bowl and the professor asked why and I said that I didn't like soup and he went on filling the other bowls acting like the father of the family.

The professor and Petra came and went serving the food, giving Rufina a break that I knew she deserved, and you know why.

Mother walked slowly over to the table and sat at the head, sipping her noodle soup noisily, her lack of teeth turning her lunch into an ordeal and a disgusting spectacle for me and maybe for the others too I don't know.

While they sipped their soup we heard plates clattering in the kitchen and the voices of Petra and the professor and I told Rufina that the time had come for our entrance and we excused ourselves and went to the kitchen and I asked why Petra was looking so red and the professor who was standing stock still and silent and Petra said, It's your turn to speak and then Rufina to bring an end to this unpleasant business. I addressed the professor known as José Camaleón directly accusing him of raping a disabled minor who was now seven months pregnant and he said Betina is eighteen and he thought she wasn't a minor but I said she was and when it came to being handicapped a judge just had to look at her and he'd go straight to jail and it would be on the front page of the newspapers and Petra hit him in the face with a slotted spoon drawing blood which he cleaned with a dishcloth and Rufina, lying, said that Betina had told her that he'd grabbed her like an animal and had made her privates hurt and she hadn't menstruated since then and we said that we were going to report him to the police unless he, during dessert and toasting with champagne, announced the marriage between him and Betina and the professor said that he had a girlfriend who was Anita and Petra hit him again with the spoon, knocking him down onto a kitchen stool.

The person I had allowed into the house was a scoundrel, he had helped me but that was ancient history, today's events were contemporary history and the professor saw himself dismissed from his position and worse arrested as a pedophile. (I barely ever use the dictionary anymore).

Let me think . . . let me think, begged the person or professor who from now on I shall call person and the three of us answered no, it had all been decided and we'd made an appointment at city hall for November 2 and I thought, My, my, it's the day of the dead, and we were already halfway through October and Betina was coming into her eighth month and the person asked if we gave his name and we informed him that we had arranged a civil wedding for the following November 2 advised by a notary friend who would make sure that it was carried out properly, and the person bit back his refusal and agreed, and Petra said, You son of a bitch, don't even think of running because the police have been informed and the precinct captain is a friend of mine.

The Second Toast

Petra had copied the telephone number and address of Abalorio de los Santos Apóstoles and his girlfriend Anita del Porte who the person now said was his girlfriend and we agreed to call and invite them to the toast with some excuse, we'd think of something, my birthday maybe. We had to surround the subject José Camaleón on all sides—and we would—and Petra said that after he married Betina he could go to hell.

Betina was brought in dressed up like a little girl, in pink taffeta and with ribbons that pulled her sparse blond hair to either side. Her childish buckle shoes were white and matched her short white socks; she barely had any legs and I felt a mortal sorrow that I didn't let overwhelm me because I had the bride's engagement ring in my pocket that at the proper time the groom would give her along with the ceremonial words of commitment.

In the new chair helped by Mother who was looking more human, Betina tried to protect her little dress with a pink napkin tied around the neck and her little eyes shone because she was wearing lipstick and her incredibly deformed nails were varnished.

The plates were brought out by Petra and Rufina who had played her part. The person ate reluctantly and as the time for the toast approached they brought out the two bottles of champagne given to us by the cousins who had come and gone right away, whose names I never got, but I learned later who they were because Mother said that they'd been dead for twenty years even though I insisted I'd seen them and the two bottles had been kept by Petra but we never spoke of it again.

Petra kept an attentive eye on the door because the moment for the solemn toast was approaching and the couple Anita and Abalorio hadn't yet arrived and when they did they brought a little gift for the birthday girl, me, which I took and thanked them for before going to put it in my room. All were seated formally and Petra and I, who had seen them together at a formal occasion once and then saw Anita you know when, didn't take our eyes off her or the person who was about to declare himself a fiancé who was as pale as a museum skull.

The end of everything is dessert. I once thought when

looking at a dead gentleman in a coffin enveloped by the big embroidered napkin, or whatever it is, that he looked like a dessert being served up to someone, and I learned that *cadaver* means flesh given to the worms and said to myself that he was a grand dessert, the gentleman wrapped in the grand napkin, but I know that I'm mischievous and one shouldn't make fun of pious customs and I'm sorry but that's what the dead look like—an offering. When I die I've already asked to be cremated because worms disgust me even though they never asked to be born worms but they still make me sick and Betina's dessert reminded me of the posthumous packaging of that good gentleman and they started to cut the cake.

Petra went to fetch the bottles of champagne that she'd kept ready to open when someone got married she certainly didn't expect it to be Betina and I helped her to fill the glasses and suggested a toast and raising my glass I said, We're going to toast Betina's marriage to Professor José Camaleón which will take place in a civil ceremony on November 2 at eleven in the morning at the Register Office, and as I'd already given the groom the little ring he put his hand in his pocket and slipped it onto the ring finger of the left hand of the bride and kissed her lightly on the cheek and she cried yes . . . yes . . . yes . . .

And I continued with my congratulations saying Betina would be a mother soon and if they looked at her belly they'd see that it was quite imminent and although the groom was a little old they'd still be happy and at that moment Anita fainted into Abalorio de los Santos Apóstoles's arms but he couldn't keep her up because she was taller and heavier than he and they both fell to the floor with a great crash and broke two glasses.

Anita del Porte got up and so did Abalorio who innocently thought she was overcome with emotion and they decided to leave in her old car and Betina continued to cry yes . . . yes . . . yes . . .

Mother had fallen asleep and I don't think she was aware of anything because she had taken sedative pills, Rufina, Petra, and I drank almost all the champagne from the mysterious cousins who'd brought the bottles and left, and who according to mother had been dead for a long time, so it could never have been them who'd brought the bottles. Rufina and the professor person cleared the table, Rufina singing as she went.

Now, I said to the fiancé, you have to carry Betina to the bedroom I gave her and you'll see that the bed is for two and as you're practically married you can sleep with her and take care of her during the night to give Rufina a break.

Betina lifted her pseudopodia with ungulated hands and fingers for the fiancé to lift her up and take her to the bedroom and Rufina called after him to clean the chair thing which she wouldn't do anymore because a couple must take care of each other and what was in the receptacle under the chair was sizable because as she grew up everything the handicapped woman did grew too and he had fixed obligations and when he went to give his classes if he wanted her to clean Mrs. Betina he'd have to pay her because she worked for one family not two and the fiancé said yes to everything with Betina in his arms before taking Betina to her new bedroom and exhausted by all the work and excitement he dropped down next to Betina after covering her with a blanket and fell asleep.

At the Register Office

Everything comes and everything goes, and I think that Betina's baby will come and go and when I say go it makes me shudder like the shudder my mother has which got worse after her retirement and almost the whole family—if not the whole family—suffers from trembling or Parkinson's disease, horrible. We have the whole set I think the only thing we lack is a little celestial charity, the charity the catechism priest talked about, and then November 2 came around.

At eight in the morning, Rufina, Petra, and I were up, first we used the bathroom that the groom had already used because he'd gone to give his classes and would come back at ten.

Finally we fixed up Betina so she'd look fresh and see if we could stop her from doing the business you know about all over herself because we wanted to take her without her chair . . . but how . . .

We didn't bother with Mother because she was in such a stupor—she lived on another planet—so we didn't wake her up.

In addition we let Abalorio de los Santos Apóstoles and his partner Anita del Porte Cavallero know that we'd signed them up to act as witnesses and they agreed by telephone.

I thought that the party would go to the Register Office in two cars, Anita del Porte Cavallero's being one of them, I add that she requested the additional surname because she thought it sounded dignified and I thought that if she married Abalorio her business card would be as long as a concertina—Anita del Porte Cavallero de De los Santos Apóstoles—and told her so and she informed me that her divorce proceedings weren't complete and so although she was separated she continued to use her husband's surname which was Bragettini Méndez, and so she'd have to be patient, and I warned her that if by chance she'd had other ideas that were related to my future brother-in-law she needed to forget them or Petra and I would wipe them out for her and the woman with green eyes called me a slum urchin but that didn't affect me because the poor people of the slums are generally good and she lived with a poor fellow who she was cheating on now and would again and I felt sorry for the docile or whatever he was Abalorio de los Santos Apóstoles to which I added an Amen.

At ten in the morning my future brother-in-law arrived dressed as a groom and wearing Atkinson cologne. Petra was wearing a striped outfit that made her look taller and a Tirolese hat that also enhanced her height, Rufina was wearing a dress of thick fabric with a fur collar and gloves and I wore an English Prince of Wales outfit and the two of us wore low heels. Petra wore stilettos. My hat crushed my wavy hair so I took it off. I forgot to say that Rufina wasn't wearing a hat either because she'd got a perm and wanted to show it off.

We dressed the little bride in a long dress of very delicate fabric, white shoes, and silk stockings with a short lace veil and we made her up—but not much, it was very discreet.

We were doing this when the telephone rang and the witnesses informed us that they'd meet us at the Register Office at the appointed time and we all appeared at the appointed time and the lady at the Register Office was already there and couldn't conceal a little amazement when she saw Betina in the groom's arms because Petra and I were of the firm opinion that a chair in the Register Office was bad luck and the brother-in-law obeyed our instructions exactly.

To the formal questions of agreement or otherwise, the brother-in-law answered yes and so did Betina and she spoke so normally that the lady from the Register Office smiled, thinking that the girl only suffered from somatic deficiencies, and then the couple signed their names but Betina did have trouble with this because she hadn't even got through third grade. But Petra and I made her practice for several days beforehand and at the end the witnesses said they were in a hurry and had to go into the city and we went home without celebrating because Betina had dirtied her little dress and his perfumed jacket.

I decided to head out to do what I always did, to paint at the School of Fine Art, eat in a little café on the Pasaje Dardo Rocha, and forget that I'd ever known Professor José Camaleón in a an effort to improve myself as much as possible in order to survive and in any case whenever I got a few pesos together I'd buy a one-room apartment and if Petra wanted she could come live with me because I felt that Petra was the best of that hovel of babbled words, shuddering, drooling, and memories of being hit with a pointer in childhood by a soulless mother a disappeared father and now the new mismatched couple . . .

I shall try to learn to use commas and periods because everything I write falls down on top of me like a spilled bowl of alphabet soup and the reader might well feel the same way but I can't do everything all at once and I also have to learn about capital letters and apostrophes. I only finished sixth grade but thanks to my artistic ability I now go to concerts and artistic gatherings and I have won several prizes for painting.

Sometimes I remember how I jumped on the professor who's now my brother-in-law when he congratulated me and encouraged me but events happened like an unexpected shooting and I don't think I've been ungrateful to the professor because Betina deserves to be respected and I learned that inside an apparently kindly person an awful pedophilic monster might be lurking and here I close another wound in addition to many more I've never spoken about because it's as though the things you don't talk about never happened.

It was evening and I was still in the café when Petra arrived and told me that Mother wasn't feeling well and she'd been taken to the clinic.

Well, I said, be patient . . . come have dinner with me, then we'll see how things are.

Mother died at the clinic and we had her taken straight to the funeral home the proper way.

Then we went with her to the cemetery and watched them shovel dirt onto her coffin.

Betina's Due Date

I had decided to ignore everything that went on at home, which I now thought of as belonging to Betina, the wife and future mother. Petra said, Don't get upset, Yuna, wait to see how Betina gets through the birth, if she does . . . and I almost slapped her because it had never occurred to me that something could happen to Betina other than give birth the way all women did but Petra explained that my sister was very different to other women and that we should do the paperwork concerning my mother's legacy given that a stranger was among us. We found a friendly lawyer who gave us the titles and documents that asserted my ownership of the meager assets and property and here Petra said that given Betina's enormous handicap everything would belong to me and to leave things in her hands because thanks to her practice of the oldest profession she had powerful contacts. And I agreed.

I'm going to write about something that happened quite a while ago when I was looking for eggs in the grass that I could never forget and it's the only cruel thing I've ever done.

A chrysalis was stuck to the rough bark of a tree, summer was still a long way off and it was a cold afternoon, so I mischievously began to blow on my hands to warm up the air around the chrysalis and watched as after a while the chrysalis opened up and out came a pink baby worm and I stopped blowing and the worm froze to death, deceived by my evil scheme and if it weren't for that when warm weather came it would have been a butterfly and I realized that I had committed a crime against nature and cried all night for several nights.

It was fading from my memory but for some reason when Betina was taken to the hospital it came back like it had just happened but nothing happens by chance and everything has a common root and as you can see I've almost mastered language although I fall down in places but step by step I'm making progress. Bear with me because I'm still talking about Betina and I wasn't there when she was taken to the clinic and her husband, my brother-in-law and the father of the child, took her and Rufina went too and when we heard, Petra and I went as well but we stayed sitting in the corridor and didn't get very close because we were very upset and saw a nurse come out of the delivery room with bloody sheets and run down the hall.

The story of the pink caterpillar that had been victim of the elements was the only thing I could think about and it drowned out a lullaby by Brahms which was playing from a music box I'd bought to give to Betina when the newborn baby cried so she could put it to sleep with the lovely melody. But the melody got interrupted as suddenly as though the box I was keeping had blown up in my hands and my brother-in-law came out of the delivery room like he'd been blasted out and he was crying.

Petra and I didn't say anything and the man cried, drying his tears with a very ordinary checked handkerchief and I went over to him, he tried to hug me but I rejected him and he told me and Petra too that the baby had been born, cried a little, and then died because the doctor said it was premature and had suffered from certain deformations. But what about Betina?

Betina was very weak and they assumed that she didn't realize that she'd lost the baby and it would be better not to tell her until she'd recovered . . . or who knows what . . .

Too many whats . . .

Petra wanted to see Betina and I followed her still shrouded in the memory of my crime in the countryside like I was trapped inside a frame and couldn't get out and Petra sobbed like a peasant, so hard that they asked her to be quiet so as not to disturb the seriously ill patients and she spat back that the sickest person was Betina and they scolded her again and she went quiet and so we went into the delivery room where it looked like Betina was hanging from plastic vines down which flowed blood and other liquids and I say vines remembering the countryside I mentioned, but they didn't show us the baby.

I walked away and made a friendly face at a nurse to whom I gave fifty pesos to tell me more about the baby saying it was my nephew and she brought a jar in which floated something approximating a baby but not quite and I asked her if they had the right to treat a newborn like that and the woman said that as an interesting specimen for study they did, especially with the father's permission. The mother didn't count because she was completely handicapped and she walked down the hall with her anatomical exhibit which would be a study aid in neonatology classes.

Petra wanted to complain but I stopped her because we'd already had too many funerals and there was no doubt that the thing floating in the laboratory jar was worthy of being on our heraldic crest and look at the impressive vocabulary I've mastered thanks to the dictionary.

They said that Betina would have to stay in the hospital for several days and I ignored them because I'd already done plenty. It was up to the father now and Petra agreed but not Rufina who didn't have anywhere to go other than the house that once belonged to mother and would now be mine and

Betina's too I suppose, although I'd be keeping that absolutely to myself.

We left the clinic and along with it the husband and wife and Rufina. Petra and I would go to dinner, then to the cinema, and then we'd look for somewhere to rent until I had enough to buy a small one-room apartment.

Winter Color

It was raining as we left the bar and pouring when we got to the restaurant. We were experiencing absurd weather that seemed to have lost its way in the calendar because by the end of November it's supposed to be summer, but in the city the unexpected downpours drive you crazy and if you've taken an umbrella with you, you won't need it and if you don't wear a coat you'll freeze but if you do you'll boil . . . this city of ours exposed to all the winds that alter the temperatures so if you're inclined to walk or sit on a bench in the middle of the square to think or go through the woods and dig into the top layer of mud with your toe you'll feel archaic dampness, as though the city of La Plata had been forcibly built on unsuitable terrain for political reasons or whatever. History never stayed with me and all I know is I like this dank threatening city in which we are united not by love but horror like in the verse by Jorge Luis Borges the poet who seduces me with how he expresses himself which is remotely similar to how I express myself or rather my way is similar to his out of respect. I once saw him out walking with his cane stumbling on the cobbles of Buenos Aires staring out with empty dead eyes which scared me and I thought that it wasn't Borges but the ghost of Borges and I crossed the street because I could see his soul was slipping away and dragging mournfully along and then he died on a trip and he's not in the country anymore because he's buried in Switzerland.

And that figure drenched in the rain, I think, so resembled my own sorrows that it made me tremble as if I suffered from the family's Parkinson's disease. After that the sweet ghost never visited me again because he didn't know me and it's one of the losses I regret but right now I was with Petra.

We went to dinner close by the railway station and then in a nearby hotel asked for a room to sleep in because I didn't want to go home. And we washed in a comfortable bathroom and woke up and had breakfast right there but on the ground floor and then we arranged with the gentleman at the hotel that we'd come back because we were looking for a permanent abode to set ourselves up in and Petra who was very knowledgeable took me to an agency where they offered quite cheap rents not very far from the city center and I said to Petra let's go to the bank where I had my savings to take out enough for a month's rent and then we'd see.

We chose a one-room apartment, already furnished. I paid the agreed price and Petra went home to fetch clothes and my papers, cardboards, canvases, and everything else, Petra always remembered everything and went to her house to let her mother, Aunt Ingrazia, know about our decision and she told me that her father, Uncle Danielito, insisted that we could live with them and she agreed to mention it to me which she did and I said that if Petra wanted to stay with her parents she could but I wasn't leaving the apartment and Petra gladly agreed to stay with me and we set about putting everything away and then I started to paint a canvas I'd already begun about the disasters you know about.

And then, when the owner came I told him that I'd like to buy the property and when he saw the canvas he recognized Yuna Riglos and exclaimed, my goodness of course . . . He suggested that he buy the painting when it was finished because he painted too but just as a hobby, he had no pretentions.

Sometimes I have been unexpectedly lucky and that was what happened with the apartment where the owner and amateur painter removed the furniture that was there and I brought mine, which wasn't very much and the painting table and everything else fit.

We were hit by a week of autumnal rain that worsened the

burden of memory and we each started on our daily routine and the only thing I asked of Petra was that she never mention the recent past because I wanted to feel as though I had newly arrived in the world, as though I had hatched out of a big egg, I wanted to be a different kind of bird. Which do you want to be, Petra asked, and I chose a sparrow that comes and goes and never stops in one place for long and she could do what she liked and we wouldn't waste the money we earned however and we shouldn't worry about anyone around us because we were all that mattered and she understood and called me wise and said she'd always listen to me and I said that I would to her but that we shouldn't feel like Siamese twins and I explained what that was and she understood again.

We'd open a separate account in the bank into which we'd make deposits every month and end up buying the apartment and Petra agreed to that too.

As I was painting one evening the owner of the apartment appeared and asked permission to sit down and I told him not to speak because he would interrupt me and the good gentleman did as he was told and when Petra came back he invited us to dinner, which meant we'd save some money.

But I still had to go to the School of Fine Art and the first time I came across my brother-in-law a cold shiver ran down my spine that I hid when my brother-in-law José Camaleón came over I went stiff as a board and he said something to me that I didn't understand because when I don't want to hear things I don't and the professor bowed his head and continued walking to the classroom and I counted the months I had left until I finished my final course, which was two and I wouldn't have to pass by the place I had loved so much, not even the corner it was on. And I thought about how I had used the word *loved*, it was the first time I had used it and I continued on my way in the opposite direction from Professor José Camaleón. I never found out what he said to me and neither did I care.

My paintings which were wanted by important galleries and exhibition venues drove the owner of the apartment where Petra and I lived crazy and he suggested waiving the rest of what was required to purchase the property if I allowed him to purchase a canvas entitled *Willows in Winter*. Of course I agreed and Petra brought a notary, the you-know-what customer of hers, and it was all formally done in the notary's office and the notary congratulated the former owner of the property for choosing a Riglos and he believed it was a profitable deal and suggested that he install air-conditioning in the apartment and the gentleman former owner agreed and we all went to dinner at a restaurant near the racetrack to celebrate.

The gentleman former owner deserves a description for his great kindness and he'll never know how many problems he took care of for me. The gentleman was middling in stature and very dark skinned, the typical businessman although in his case he was a little bit artist too which may sound strange but it was true and he always dressed well in different suits, and shirts, ties, designer shoes (you could tell) and all top quality with a garish Chevalier ring on his little finger which he waved around too much to allow the light to hit it properly.

He had two cars and don't ask me what type because I don't know anything about cars and when he invited us out he drove us in the nicest one because he wanted to impress us, not me but Petra. I told Petra that I didn't want trouble with this gentleman and for her to restrain herself because otherwise the gentleman would lose respect for us. And if she ever considered doing something out of place it didn't show at all and when the invitations began to flood in I started to make excuses about work and so they slowed. But the gentleman whose nickname was Cacho still came in the evenings to watch me paint and I suggested that I paint him but that he shouldn't expect the painting to be ordinary but in my style and he agreed excitedly and kissed my hand. I washed it afterward.

And Cacho came on Fridays at seven in the evening to pose. He came in a white suit and pink shirt over which was draped a white tie. The shoes were white too. I would stylize the outfit, his Italian face his chubby worker's hands and the pose they take, thinking, those who were born poor but got rich without rising to a certain social level they can only dream of, of posterity. I would make the good Cacho Spichafoco, his surname, anew and he said he would adore me like gleaming Venus, I was already a part of a respectable cultural scene so much so that at the School of Fine Art they offered me substitute teaching places because Professor José Camaleón was retiring. I agreed because I had now mastered the spoken word and would try to speak as little and paint as much as possible.

A New Friendship That May Well Last

Cacho, whose name was Carmelo, and you already know the
surname which made me think of a dragon breathing fire, arrived
punctually to pose after I'd given my first class at the School of
Fine Art, which went well and I thought about my words and
phrases before I said them, just like my imagined Spichafoco
dragon. The class wasn't very big so I was bold enough to write
some relevant expressions in colored chalk regarding the styles
and techniques of artists in different periods and was moved to
see the students taking notes with serious-minded respect, but I
must confess that when the bell rang I sighed in relief, although
after the first class it would be easier to teach the course in a
relaxed way without inner, hidden fears that might burst out at
any moment, which would reveal to the students that the person

trying to teach them was a reeducated handicapped woman and then they'd take advantage of my natural disadvantage.

What wonderful youth, I thought to myself, healthy and malleable as newly grown reeds by the river, pale or rosy and what naturally human eyes in faces well born so prepared for the task and what hands . . . I'd paint a canvas under the spell of this small group of angels, fairies and little courtly knights who reminded me of engravings and paintings from the museums I had visited and glossy art books with characters no doubt born to a human couple in love without the lust or incest that wither the fruit on the branch watered repeatedly by filthy swampy blood. And so I watched them stride confidently out onto the street, in control of their lives, while I returned to the boneyard, my familiar funereal state of mind.

I'd have to tame the hairy beast that scratched at my insides because I wasn't an exception but did have an opportunity to escape a grotesque circus, my ill-crossed fate, an ocean of exhausted, moribund liquids. Yes, I had to triumph over all that awful excrement and deformity and I would so long as I could call on the vital energies of my youth. The effort wasn't insignificant but required hours spent awake clinging on to the words in books not just about literature and art but also the anatomical sciences, and supposedly chance conversations with people who had experience with abnormality. So my life went on and every class or meeting with students and professors meant great effort and fear, and afterward a sigh of relief because no one had noticed my impediments only just overcome, and the quality of my paintings which were worth more year upon year and were discussed at length alongside other extremely valuable works. But I could never forget my fear of failure because I was descended from degenerate, damaged genes.

Cacho saw how tired I was and I told him I'd just given a class and let's go to a café for a cool drink, I'd pay. Cacho or Carmelo cried out not at all, he'd pay, and we went out. I ordered a ham sandwich and a soda and Carmelo ordered cognac with the glass heated up first and I realized that he was trying to show off his class. He asked whether I liked cognac and I answered that I never drank alcohol. We then went back to the apartment where Petra was making dinner. A bizarre expression appeared on Carmelo's recently shaven face with its trimmed mustache that almost made me burst out laughing, but I held it back. I painted for quite a while. The sooner I finished the portrait the better because the classes needed hours of preparation, so I painted Carmelo-Cacho just as he was, although with a more elegant expression and features. I promised him that the portrait would be ready the following week and covered it with a cloth. But the shy model didn't ask to see it.

Petra was still making a simple meal of beef and ravioli. She'd bought dessert at La Paris, the closest patisserie to us, and called me so I went to the kitchen and Petra asked if she could invite Cacho. I said yes but not to invite him again and regarding invitations in general the gentleman's were more than enough already. Petra understood. Later we'd have a serious discussion.

Petra invited the now silent Cacho or Carmelo, who accepted. I noticed how happy he looked and he asked permission to buy wine or champagne. I said that we didn't drink but Petra who did drink looked disappointed but he insisted because the aroma of the ravioli was too enticing to his Italian soul not to have a glass or two and I couldn't object but I said to Petra don't drink alcohol and never contradict my wishes, I know what I'm doing, and she agreed.

We started to eat dinner and Carmelo praised the ravioli for which Petra said she'd made the vegetable filling herself along with the sauce but I knew that in the trash bag was the box of store-bought ravioli and the little carton of sauce and sensed that the Lilliputian whose mischievousness was several feet taller than she was was plotting something and Carmelo took some bread from the basket and dipped it, praising the flavor which he said reminded him of the sauce his *mamma italiana* made because the Spichafocos were Sicilian and very fond of pasta, and he eagerly devoured the culinary masterpiece by Petra who didn't know that it was dangerous to lie to a Sicilian, even if it is only about pasta. Later when the repast was complete we would clear up several murky points. Readers will be amazed at my progress with writing although I still make mistakes with my punctuation but I promise to correct the punctuation and you must forgive me because one can't do everything at once and in a short time I've run as far as a marathon. I believe I am cultured. And I shall grow more cultured as far as the weaknesses in my nature allow.

It so happened that we turned on the radio to listen to the news and Carmelo asked whether we had a television and I said we didn't but not to even think about it and Petra asked, Why not? Enough, I said quite seriously.

There wasn't any room for a television because I took up a lot of space with my table and paintings and there was only just enough for the two little beds one for me the other for Petra and the chairs and the table where I ate occasionally because I preferred to eat in the café and who knows where Petra preferred.

A television is a tyrant that would keep Petra stuck in front of it without doing anything and I had to work on my courses and paintings. There's no room here, I insisted and explained, and the subject didn't come up again.

We listened to the radio for a while and Carmelo gratefully said his goodbyes. I looked at Petra's expression. I wasn't about to complicate my life for anything in the world.

I told Petra that we needed to discuss the issue seriously and had no trouble naming it, Cacho Carmelo Spichafoco, because that was what we'd talk about to clear everything up down to the last detail, details like the periods and commas I need to learn to put in their rightful places. And we'd do it over a friendly cappuccino. Petra was a little haughty and I didn't like that.

Petra, I said, Mr. Cacho Carmelo Spichafoco has completed the sale of the apartment and I don't want him as a friend because I don't know anything about the life of Mr. Cacho Carmelo Spichafoco and before he starts to take liberties I hope to show him that our interaction was only related to the apartment and that he shouldn't be so forward as to offer significant gifts because we're working people who earn their living with the sweat from whatever sweats—you know what I mean—don't think, Petra, that I have forgotten the atrocities you're capable of and I'm not criticizing but the gentleman is Italian and from the island of Sicily and you don't mess around with people like that because they're very good but if you cross them you can forget about seeing the day following your mistake. Why did you lie about the ravioli and the sauce, you're flirting with the gentleman and that's dangerous, I know what I'm talking about and I'm not getting you out of any more trouble—you know what I mean—and the gentleman will come by next week for the portrait that I shall give him to end the chain of gratitude or debt if any existed.

Petra's miniature form slumped and she started to weep. I told her that we'd never been more comfortable and had to go

on that way but as I wasn't used to forcing my opinion on anyone, because my nature was not despotic, if she had other op-
tions and wanted to diverge from my way of living she should
let me know immediately.

Petra Decides

We went to bed and I immediately heard Petra snoring and realized that my proposal that she be more disciplined in the future had not hit home.

Lying on my pillow in the faint moonlight that filtered in through the windows I saw the little woman who was nonetheless a hindrance because she kept me up and I needed to sleep all night to work all day.

Petra was free of judgment or perhaps she was incapable of reflecting on how awful her deeds were, placing her so-called work on the same level as my work even though it earned only what her clientele wanted to pay. The bruises and bites and suck marks on her neck helped her to find other customers by informing them of the nature of her exploits, because she couldn't cover the marks on her neck with makeup, shawls, or scarves, and laid bare her immorality, what she really was. What cruel people she dealt with and the poor thing was unwittingly heading down a slope further each week after the most heated but best-paid encounters. Though I did before, I didn't recognize this servile dreg of humanity now that I had worked so hard to gain ground with the written word and was in my final year at the School of Fine Art and thanks to the quality of my paintings had been given the honor of taking extra classes for younger students with excellent results. Where to place this pitiful human, or almost human mouse, whom I had always helped and who was bound to my not so normal humanity, whom I saved from prison but never tried to save from her dark life of groping and sinful embraces with old degenerates married and single and who knows what else . . . Had I done a lot or not enough for Petra? I didn't know and never will.

And in the middle of the moonlight moon-bright night I saw the little human mouse eyes staring at me and tried to pretend to be asleep but she declared that she knew what I was thinking and said that if I asked she'd gather her things and disappear right away and I needn't worry because she'd go to live with her parents, with Aunt Ingrazia and Uncle Danielito even if the most brutal incidents of her past jumped over the wall or climbed the other way and Carina's soul tormented her with who knows what horrors but just one word from me would decide her future and I told her to go to sleep I wasn't sleepy and would finish the portrait of Cacho Carmelo and she hugged the pillow and started to snore right away, her consciousness was so fragile, her subconscious so receptive.

But that wasn't true of me and while I cleaned my brushes late into the night in the lamplight I came up with different scenarios to propose to Petra. Because my older students would come to my atelier room and the boys, hopefully not but maybe would recognize Petra and you know from where.

And you couldn't confuse Petra with anyone else.

As dawn arrived I finished the portrait. Cacho Carmelo had come out much better than he was in real life. I emphasized the Chevalier ring on his little finger because he had suggested it and even the diamond shone out from his *contadino* paw. Petra got up and went to make a breakfast of white coffee and medialunas. I noticed that the little woman's face had aged, or perhaps it was my imagination.

She started the conversation. She told me that she had somewhere to go if she was unwelcome in the apartment, and I was quick to say that she was welcome, and she had contributed some money too and if she decided to go I would pay her back because I'd paid for almost the entire acquisition and it was all certified by the notary, to avoid misunderstandings, but it wasn't up to me to decide whether she should stay or go

although I did fill her in on potentially prejudicial consequences
that she had to understand for both our sakes.

Petra was much perkier than I had expected and as she ate
her breakfast she said that if she left she'd miss me because no
one had ever helped her like I had.

When it came to her work, the oldest in the world, it was
wearing her out and now she was afraid of the diseases going
around and she'd rather stay in my apartment but I should give
her back the little money she'd paid which was a minimal sum
so the apartment would belong to me alone which I thought
fair and I agreed to do the paperwork at the notary's office. We
went that afternoon and then I continued with my classes and
the numerous activities required of my specialty and she would
have done the same and we didn't see each other again until that
night when we had a modest supper at the café. There she asked
me humbly if she'd be sleeping in my apartment or whether she
had no right anymore in which case she'd go back to her parents' house and I said that she was still my employee and I'd
increase her salary from fifty to a hundred pesos. She was so
happy that tears came to her eyes.

The silence that followed went on for too long because we
both had more things to clear up or smooth out.

Suddenly we both started talking at once and I let her go
first. She told me that she still owed me because she hadn't
informed me of something that Aunt Ingrazia and Uncle

Danielito, which is to say her parents, my aunt and uncle, would come to tell me about the next day, at dinnertime.

A gray sheen fell over my eyes. Once again I was seeing things that others couldn't see which in my childhood and adolescence was Betina's tail which meant her soul was slipping away but then momentous events occurred and I never saw them coming.

She began to explain things but not very coherently and named her parents, Abalorio de los Santos Apóstoles and his girlfriend Ana del Porte Cavallero, I think she stopped there and asked my permission to hold a very intimate dinner in my apartment with a surprise that she was still keeping secret and that the food would come from a very well-known rotisserie in the city and there would be drinks and table service and she swore that it would be the last time she'd bother me because I was a little bothered and with good reason but she begged me like a little girl to have a little more patience and everything would become as clear as water.

I can't deny that I had to make an effort that day during classes and that the brushstrokes flashed and I felt a chaotic neurosis that I was able to drive away telling myself that whatever happened it was nothing compared to my efforts at self-improvement. I looked at the clock several times and remembered how long it took me to learn to tell the time and that old shiver ran through my skeleton and I was afraid of regressing.

The dusk arrived, crisp and silent.

Petra had been in my apartment since early on, she might not have left all day, and the floor and furniture all sparkled. The serving tables had already been delivered and the fact that my paintings, worktable, and the rest had been moved into our small storage space almost sent me into a rage but Petra promised it wouldn't happen again and I went to take a shower and to finish a painting in the storage space.

When I try to escape a harsh objective reality I enter into a stupor, and I fell asleep on top of the work and was woken by voices that were forgotten but familiar.

I went out to meet the voices and couldn't help but be amazed by both the audience and the sight, which I must say was extraordinary, of the table laid as it had been many years ago to celebrate christenings or birthdays before my father left and they'd even set up the candelabra to illuminate the feast and, why not, all the guests were dressed up, and I felt strange in the odd world that had been created while I had dozed which hadn't been for very long and I saw Petra diligently buzzing around like a wasp and also the couple consisting of Abalorio de los Santos Apóstoles and Ana del Porte and beyond them Cacho Carmelo Spichafoco and greeting the room as they came in I saw Aunt Ingrazia and Uncle Danielito . . . who was missing? Only Professor José Camaleón and his wife, Betina, who were closely related to all present except for the couple

Abalorio-Ana. Rufina came in carrying a bouquet of flowers from the professor and his wife, you know who I'm talking about, and a letter for Petra and I felt that it should be for me as the owner of the property but that was how things were.

I had the feeling that major changes were coming and I would be the last to find out but I didn't care so long as they left me in peace to do my work and live my life as I saw fit.

I greeted everyone and they greeted me and we all sat around the table each of us with their plate and cutlery and wine and water glass and chewing jaws because there was so much to eat and no one was to deprive themselves of anything. I asked what all the fuss was about.

Rufina spoke up saying that she wouldn't be taking part and had brought the flowers and card because her employers wouldn't be coming because Mrs. Betina didn't go out at night and she said her goodbyes and left. I followed her and she told me that she was thinking about going back to her home province of San Luis because the lady and gentleman could manage on their own and to forgive her but she was tired of cleaning up the mess of the poor lady who couldn't control her piss or the other and watching the poor melancholy gentleman mope around and it was time for him to start cleaning and so on because she couldn't stand it anymore. I thought that sounded reasonable.

Petra opened the envelope and read out, Dear Petra, we

wish you all the happiness in the world but we can't go to your party because we don't go out at night.

What party, Petra? I asked in surprise and Cacho Carmelo answered that he would have the honor of asking for Petra's hand from her good parents here present, which is to say Aunt Ingrazia and Uncle Danielito, and I stammered saying, Petra, why didn't you tell me, and she said to give you a pleasant surprise and I sighed.

Cacho Carmelo looked gentlemanly at everyone's expressions from left to right and found teeth bared in smiles of approval except for mine which were still in shock praying to Santa Rita my patron saint that the fiancé never find out you-know-what and explode the way that Sicilians do but then I was in for another surprise when Cacho Carmelo stood to make a speech, his champagne glass raised to toast the little lady with the big heart who had been unfortunate enough to lose her younger sister Carina and always cried over her in his arms thus showing the goodness of her heart and soul as did the fact that she chose to accompany her lonely cousin, which is to say me instead of living with her parents in the comfort of her sweet paternal home, forgive the redundancy.

I thought back to the tragedy of the potato man with his private parts in his mouth and then Petra and I rushing around to hide the evidence and cover up the truth like a pair of mimes on a diabolical stage and only now did I realize how dangerous the dwarf was. But this time I swore that I'd get myself out of the filthy tragicomedy untouched.

And the fiancé went on exultantly while the parents of the bride-to-be cried with emotion and the other relatives and nonrelatives continued smiling, saying that next year, January, because we were already in December, they'd have a church wedding and would choose San Ponciano because Ponciano was his grandfather's name.

And now, he said, putting his hand in his jacket pocket, we will get engaged with these rings and look, he said, the jewel is a diamond set in platinum and of course the bands are gold and have our names and the date, today, on the inside and I shall proceed to bejewel my fiancée and future wife and beg her to do the same. Applause and kisses. I don't remember moving from my chair because I was in shock, but I recovered because I had seen much worse and clapped from my seat.

Cacho Carmelo insisted on telling the story of their seren-dipitous love affair, and said that the civil wedding would be the morning of the first Friday of January and that night they would marry in the church and the bride would wear a dress of the best silk and lace and the train would be held by a nephew called Carmelito and then their honeymoon would be in Punta del Este.

And he thanked me for how good I had been to his future wife, he'd never forget it, and then I went to the storage space

and brought back the finished portrait which was met with an
exclamation and Cacho Carmelo congratulated me and said it's
obvious that my Chevalier is pure diamond and the others said
that he looked very handsome and he said that he was handsome enough to be worthy of his saintly little bride.

I would have preferred for it all to have been a nightmare.
But no. I counted the days that Petra had left to stay with me
hoping they'd pass quickly.

Then Petra started to speak and said that the witnesses for
both the church and the civil weddings would be the same, both
she and her beloved Cachito had thought of Aunt Ingrazia and
Uncle Danielito, which is to say my aunt and uncle but her parents, and Abalorio de los Santos Apóstoles and Anita del Porte,
and I felt that the dwarf never loved me, I felt that maybe I was
in danger being close to her and saw the fire in her ratty little
eyes which burned me and I was stung by the touch of the mortal sin of envy and decided that once the table was removed and
the apartment was left on its own, maybe while the exhausted
Petra was sleeping, I'd go to the hotel I was familiar with for
that night at least and then I'd see, and that night I sensed that
Petra could be dangerous because she'd drunk too much and
wouldn't stop staring at me.

I left late into the night and got a taxi that took me to the
hotel by the train station and they put me in the same room that
I had once stayed in with Petra and given that I had promised

to return they thought this was the moment although they were surprised that I hadn't brought any luggage and I explained to the gentleman who gave me the key that the next day I'd leave after breakfast. I barely slept and fell in and out of a half-sleep so unpleasant that it was more tiring than not sleeping at all and by now the clock read three in the morning.

The next thing I knew it was ten in the morning and I went to take a shower, not having underwear was a bother but things had happened quickly so I had to accept it and my classes began at eleven. I arranged my anatomy as best I could, they wouldn't know the difference given that I didn't wear makeup but I needed my folders and cardboard but I wouldn't be daunted and although I had now mastered vocabulary to a great degree I found that the neurosis of the previous night had tied my tongue into knots which is how I described my difficulties with the spoken word which I had almost resolved but the shock was too much especially once I had glimpsed the trash piled up deep in Petra's psyche, she was a dangerous criminal and I hope I'm wrong because when one is angry they fly off the handle at anything and I was angry but it didn't show, my natural impassiveness always hid my moods and would continue to, also it wasn't long before Petra's wedding ceremonies.

Afterward I would change the lock on my apartment and my greatest hope was to forget . . . forget and continue improving until I had overcome my original handicap as much

as possible. I wouldn't forget that. I was just another part of
the massive stratum of degenerates barely approximate to the
human race in its purest natural state.

I had breakfast and paid for my hotel stay and took a taxi to
my apartment and as I rushed in I saw Petra still in bed and got
my things without making a noise.

When I got to the School of Fine Art the building at first
looked strange to me and I sat down on a step that led up to
the second floor. I realized that another shock would plunge me
back into the shadows I'd climbed out of with so much effort
and with effort I got back up and reached my class just in time.
I don't think that any of my students saw me shaking during
the first few minutes or heard any stammered words and I returned to the world of the living that I had won for myself and
deserved.

I went to have lunch at the little café although my stomach
didn't require food, which is what happens to me when I'm anx-
ious and was drinking a nonalcoholic drink when Petra plopped
down next to me like the roof falling in and kissed me on the
cheek which wasn't done in our family and I didn't say a word.

She ordered a steak and fries along with other delicacies, she
was hungry and started to chatter away with her mouth full and
the first thing she said was that Cachito had decided that during
the time that remained before they got married she would live
in the home of the Spichafoco family because Cachito's sister, a

fine couturier, was making her wedding dress and also Cachito believed that she'd be better off moving to the country house in Adrogué and that that night she'd move to her future family's home unless I had a problem with that and I almost screamed at her but I restrained myself.

We sat there, she ate and I drank water, waiting for something more that I sensed Petra wanted to say to me and I wasn't wrong. And she said to please not invite the professor and Betina to the wedding because they weren't presentable, I had to bite my tongue to stop myself from telling her to look at herself in a standing mirror and ask whether she understood what presentable meant, she'd probably go hide her sorry figure down the nearest mouse hole. But I didn't say it. She ordered a dessert of ice cream and while she was slurping away like an ugly cat she begged me to meet Cachito that night because he had important business to discuss with me and I told her he could come at eight.

The Prejudices of Cacho Carmelo
(Cachito) Spichafoco

Petra had moved out. The atmosphere was serene and it belonged to me because I didn't owe anything to anyone and everything around me, little as it was, was my own property. Was that possible? I fell asleep on the antique sofa I had bought and in the lilac cloudscape of a peaceful sleep, and in front of the sheet that must be one's soul, a firefly flashed against the dense ink and I saw two silhouettes now in the past but not yet gone and I refused to see them, yes I refused but they insisted with the urgency of the desperate. I said very quietly, Betina and José Camaleón, and from the rancid fog of the unwanted they stared at me for a moment and the ghosts—they were ghosts to me—disappeared.

The doorbell rang at eight. I answered. Cachito was formal

and well dressed, wearing Atkinson cologne, and he looked in spite of all the preening and polishing more rustic than ever and asked permission to sit down unless, if I hadn't had dinner already, I'd like to accompany him and I told him that my stomach wasn't very well and I wouldn't be having dinner and the moment he left I'd go to bed and he said early to roost like the chickens. Like the pygmies, I answered, and the mustache that had been raised high with laughter now fell and he said, Let's cut to the chase, I thought of another joke but I held back the way I always do in time.

He crossed his legs, his short *contadino* or common legs, stroked his mustache and started to chatter about trivialities and I said, Cut to the chase.

Yes, yes, we're getting there, he took a breath. I saw that he was having trouble talking.

I felt that if he disturbed my newfound peace I'd smash a chair over his blue-black dyed head.

I didn't realize that with *pygmy* I had laid the foundations for an edifice of verbiage, let's call it, but that was what happened.

I understand, Yuna, that you are envious about the fate of your little cousin but those with a good heart will sooner or later receive help from the Heart of Jesus. After all, think what a blessed life Petra will enjoy after so much suffering, the poor thing, so good and decent in this world of artists and bohemians of which you're a part, although you have been generous with the poor girl, the example of people of the night has not been good for her, I had to work hard to help her forget all the immoral experiences that she was in danger of suffering from and she even confessed that someone tried to corrupt her and although she did not name names from the description, forgive me, I think that you tried to corrupt her on several occasions. But Petra did not accuse you, perish the thought, and perhaps whoever it was who tried to muddy her purity was another artist, which is why I beg of you not to see my future wife again, not you nor any of the flamboyant long-haired characters that surround you and if you do I shall do whatever is in my power to preserve the honor of the family and if any evil tongues try to slander Petra, well . . . And he took a Sevillian navaja out of his pocket before adding, I shall cut off their tongue.

All the trials and sorrows of my life fell like a winter storm upon the sheet you know about and I didn't say a word in my horror at the looming hand brandished by the poor fool, the only fool sorrier than me because he was now beyond saving. He left.

December, January, February passed and in March I started classes again. I felt newborn, I was able to steady myself, exhibit, and travel.

I erased. Erased. I erased everything.

An enormous melancholy flooded into my paintings and it made them worth more because people find consolation in seeing their sorrows.

I heard that Betina had died and that the professor, because of the miserable existence he had led taking care of the patient, never left the house and I remembered that the house was mine, by inheritance, but I forgot that too.

AURORA VENTURINI was born in 1921 in La Plata, Buenos Aires, Argentina. She worked as a psychologist and Rorschach test specialist at the Institute of Child Psychology, where she befriended Eva Perón. In 1948, Jorge Luis Borges awarded her the Premio Iniciación for her book *El solitario*. Following the Revolución Libertadora, she lived in exile in Paris, socializing with such French existentialists as Violette Leduc. She wrote more than thirty books. In 2007, she received *Página/12*'s New Novel Award for *Cousins*. She died in 2015 in Buenos Aires, at the age of ninety-four.

KIT MAUDE is a literary translator based in Buenos Aires. He has translated dozens of writers from Spain and Latin America for a wide variety of publishers, publications, and institutions and writes reviews and literary criticism for outlets in Argentina, the United States, and the United Kingdom.